The Amish Girl From Ohio

Stephanie Swift

Published by Trellis Publishing, 2021.

THE AMISH GIRL FROM OHIO

First edition. July 14, 2021.

Copyright © 2021 Stephanie Swift.

ISBN: 979-8224120161

Written by Stephanie Swift.

THE AMISH GIRL FROM OHIO
STEPHANIE SWIFT

Sarah Brennan wearily peeked around her side of the carriage and let her gaze drift over the surrounding countryside, which was filled to overflowing with rows upon rows of tomatoes, corn, and watermelon. It felt as if she'd been traveling for an eternity, and when one of the carriage wheels clipped a large stone, jarring her and Brian, the driver, she yelped and grabbed hold of the seat to maintain her balance.

"I apologize for the bumpy road," he said, with a chuckle. "The county workers spread new gravel on it last week, so it's a bit rough right now."

She gave him a quick sideways glance, noting the dimples in his cheeks when he laughed and the way the wind ruffled his dark brown hair. They'd barely spoken since he retrieved her from the bus terminal that morning, and she didn't know what to say. She wasn't used to talking to other men besides her younger brothers and her beau, Abraham.

"So...my *daed* tells me you're from Ohio?" he inquired. "I've never traveled there before. Actually, I don't think I've been beyond the city limits of Lancaster."

Sarah smiled. She knew he was just trying to make idle conversation to pass the time, but she was still grateful for his hospitality. If there was one thing she desperately needed at the moment, it was a kind word, even from a stranger.

"*Yah*," she replied. "I lived in Dayton with my parents and siblings. My *mamm* and *daed* passed away three weeks ago in an accident, and I was sent here to live with my aunt Hope."

Sarah sensed him looking at her, but she kept her eyes focused on the road and fields.

"I'm so sorry," he said. "Do you mind me asking what happened to your siblings?"

It wasn't her favorite topic of conversation, but she knew he was just naturally concerned and curious, like most people she'd encountered since the accident.

"They're still in Dayton. Four of my younger brothers were sent to live with my aunt Ruth and uncle Micah, and Jacob, the youngest one, who's three years old, is living with my four sisters at my grandparents' house. My brothers are helping my uncle Micah manage his dairy farm, and my sisters help my grandmother with her quilting business."

He grew quiet, and she could tell from his blank stare that the wheels were turning in his mind. When his gaze widened and jaw slacked, she stifled a laugh.

"Wait...you have *nine* siblings?" he exclaimed.

She was used to the shocked expressions when people found out about her large family, even though she couldn't quite fathom what was so interesting about it. True, her family was the biggest one in her Amish community in Dayton, but for her it was commonplace and just a part of life. Many of her friends envied her big brood of brothers and sisters, but there were some who couldn't imagine sharing a home with so many siblings. Sarah considered it a blessing.

"*Yah*, there are ten of us. I miss them so much. I hope I'll get to return to Dayton someday, but my aunt Hope needs me right now."

Sarah frowned when she considered how long it might take before she could return. Her aunt Hope was getting on in years, and with no husband or children to help her manage the farm, she was forced to reach out to family members in Dayton. Her aunt Ruth promised Sarah it would be a temporary move, but she found that hard to believe.

"When was the last time you visited?" Brian asked. "My *daed* said he hasn't laid eyes on you since you were a little girl."

Sarah squinted. She could vaguely remember traveling to Lancaster – or anywhere outside of Ohio – and she certainly couldn't recall meeting Brian and his family.

"I have no idea. I suppose I was about three or four years old."

They rounded a bend in the road, and when Brian's village come into view, the butterflies in her stomach did somersaults. Her hands began to shake, and she swallowed hard past the lump lodged in her throat.

"Everyone is anxious to see you," he remarked. "Our community is small, but we're close, and if there's anything you need, don't hesitate to let someone know. I live just a couple of houses down from Miss Hope, so I'm not far away."

Sarah gave him a bashful smile. Growing up in a house full of rough-and-tumble boys, she wasn't used to being treated like a lady by a true gentleman – except for Abraham, of course.

Sarah sighed. She missed him too – immensely.

"*Denki*, Brian. That's very kind of you."

When their eyes locked, she felt her cheeks redden before she had the chance to stop it, which made Brian grin.

"Do you have someone waiting for you back home? A boyfriend or fiancé?"

Her face burned even hotter and Sarah turned her attention elsewhere to keep him from noticing.

"*Yah*, I have a boyfriend. His name is Abraham."

He didn't respond right away, but when he did Sarah could sense a change in his tone of voice.

"Well, we have a community phone near the church, and the mailman makes his rounds here around noon Monday through Saturday, so you should be able to keep in touch."

They rode the rest of the way in silence, and as Sarah took in the sights around her, she lifted her chin and tried to appear more self-confident than she felt. Before leaving Dayton, she and Abraham had a long conversation about the move, and although he promised the distance between them wouldn't change things, she could also tell he was hesitant about it, which made her nervous.

They'd been courting only a couple of months, and she hated doing anything that might jeopardize their relationship. Unfortunately, though, this was out of her hands from the beginning. All she could do was hope and pray that *Gott* would somehow keep her close to his heart.

* * * *

The sky may have been overcast, but Brian was determined to keep it from dampening his spirits. It was the third Saturday of the month, when everyone gathered at church for a rousing sermon from his father, followed by an afternoon spent eating, playing games, and fellowshipping outside. It was the one day of the month he really looked forward to and now there was a whole new reason for his excitement – Sarah.

Brian cast a brief glance across the sanctuary, where the women were seated on the opposite side from the men, and his heart leapt in his throat when he saw Sarah sitting near the front beside her aunt Hope. Her hands were folded on top of her lap and she smiled weakly and barely lifted her head when someone spoke to her.

A part of him ached for Sarah, because he knew it couldn't be easy leaving her family behind in Ohio and moving to a place where she was practically a stranger. Although he and his neighbors had done everything possible to make her feel welcome since her arrival two weeks prior, he could see the sadness etched on her beautiful face.

His father, the town Bishop, took his place behind the tall wooden podium and the next two hours were spent singing hymns and worshiping. But when the last "amen" was spoken, he honestly couldn't remember a word of his father's sermon. He felt guilty about it, but he couldn't help it either. Sarah had taken precedence in his mind since he saw her sitting alone on a bench outside the bus terminal, and he didn't know how to control it – or even if he wanted to. There was just one problem – Abraham. He had no idea if they were keeping in touch, and even though he was dying to find out, he wasn't about to start snooping.

When the congregation stood to leave, Brian made a beeline for Sarah, but he'd taken barely five steps when his vision was suddenly obscured with bouncy red curls and freckles.

"*Hallo* Brian!"

Meredith Miller, a childhood friend who was one year younger than Brian, flashed him a big toothy grin and blocked his path, and he groaned when he saw Sarah making her way to the door.

"*Guder nammidaag*, Meredith. If you'll excuse me, I need to help the other men set the tables up outside so we can eat lunch."

He hoped that would appease her, but she put a hand on his chest to stop him when he tried to sidestep her. She leaned in close, and Brian instinctively took a step back.

"I just want you to know that I baked a peach pie especially for you," she whispered. "I hope you'll share it with me in the grove."

If it wasn't such an ungentlemanly thing to do, Brian would've laughed, but he knew that wouldn't be the Christian way to act either. If only Meredith wasn't so persistent. She'd been on his heels since they were six years old, and even though he'd told her repeatedly they couldn't be more than friends, she wouldn't be swayed.

"Brian!"

His *daed's* booming voice was a welcome reprieve, and when he turned to find him standing near the exit, waving for him to follow, he escaped as quickly as possible. Outside, the men were busy unloading tables and chairs from wagons while the women tended to the food. The teenagers in the group were setting up nets for badminton and volleyball, while the younger kids played hide-and-seek, and it was far too crowded and chaotic to try and pinpoint where Sarah was.

"Looking for someone in particular?" his *daed* inquired.

The two of them picked up one of the tables, and as they carried it to a group of elderly women who were unpacking desserts, Brian didn't miss his *daed's* mischievous grin. It wasn't the first time he'd tried to steer the conversation to Sarah, but Brian didn't see the point of getting his hopes up when the fact remained she was dating someone else.

"*Neh*, just seeing what everyone is doing," he replied.

His *daed* nodded, but he didn't look convinced, and as they finished setting up tables, he made it a point to keep his eyes focused on the task at hand. Once the tables were in position and the food was dispersed, everyone joined hands in a circle and Brian's *daed* led them in a prayer. As soon as he finished, they all made a mad dash for the feast.

He finally spotted Sarah in the crowd, and as he slowly edged his way closer to her, he took a deep breath to try and calm his nerves. She looked beautiful in a light blue dress that matched her eyes, and her brown hair was tied loosely at the nape of her neck with a blue ribbon. Her complexion was smooth and flawless, and when he approached her, he was delighted to see her smile.

"You may have to fight your way through if you hope to eat anything," he teased. "These people don't let anything come between them and food, especially Mrs. Judith's apple pies."

She laughed softly, and the sweet sound warmed his blood and made him weak in the knees.

"I can wait," she replied. "Don't forget I grew up with nine siblings, so I'm used to taking turns."

Brian laughed. The line to the food was slow, but he didn't mind, especially if that meant more time to talk to Sarah.

"Have you heard from them since you arrived?"

His question made her smile even brighter. "*Yah*! I received a letter yesterday from my sister, Naomi, and they're all doing really well. She said they hope to come visit soon. It was so good hearing from her, and it helps me worry less knowing they're okay."

He could understand that.

"How about Abraham? Is he doing okay too?"

Brian's cheeks burned and he groaned. The question came out before he could rationally think it through, and he wished he could take it back. He didn't want to appear nosey but, fortunately, Sarah didn't seem fazed by his question. She picked up a paper plate and began loading it with food, with barely a glance in his direction.

"I'm not sure," she responded. "I haven't heard from him yet."

If Abraham's silence bothered her, she didn't show it, but Brian could sense a bit of frustration in her tone. As they piled their plates high with delicacies, he didn't ask anymore questions, and when a couple of the women grabbed her attention and asked if she'd like to come sit with them, Brian bit his tongue and went in the opposite direction, where his parents were seated with their next-door neighbors, the Olsen's.

He tried to get involved in the conversation his *daed* and Mr. Olsen were having over some repairs that needed to be done to the church, but he couldn't tear his gaze – or his thoughts – away from Sarah. He did his best not to stare, but when the opportunity arose, he looked her way quickly and was thrilled when he caught her looking his way too.

A few minutes into the meal, Miss Hope joined her, and when she reached inside her apron pocket and pulled out a white envelope, Brian's heart sank. He feared his worst suspicion was true when Sarah smiled happily and clapped her hands together excitedly as soon as she saw who it was from.

Abraham.

Brian pushed his plate away, unable to eat another bite. Even the name made him sick to his stomach, and he didn't even know the man. He watched from afar as Sarah hastily pulled the letter from the envelope and began devouring every word, but when her smile suddenly faded, the tiny hairs on the back of his neck stood at attention.

He wanted to go to her, thinking he may have been mistaken and it was bad news from one of her siblings, but he kept his place. Sarah finished reading the letter and slowly slid it back inside the envelope. When she stood, Brian stood too, but before he could reach her, she was joined by two teenagers. They were holding badminton rackets, and within a matter of seconds, they were pulling Sarah toward the field where the net awaited.

She didn't look pleased at all.

Brian tossed his plate and cup in a nearby garbage can and started jogging toward the field. His plan was to save her from a game she obviously didn't want to play, but before he had the chance to intervene, he was also dragged into the game by two other excited – and very pushy – teenagers.

He was put on the same side as Sarah, and when he stole a few seconds to talk to her before the game started, he noticed there were unshed tears in the corners of her eyes.

"Is something wrong, Sarah?"

The other team launched the shuttle over the net before she had the chance to reply and soon they were all caught up in a fierce game of badminton that lasted far too long for his liking. There was plenty of laughter all around throughout the game, but Sarah remained oddly stoic and resigned.

Near the end of the game, when the other team served, there was a break in the gray clouds and the sun appeared for a brief moment. Sarah went to hit the shuttle back over the net, but a bright stream of sunlight shone down and temporarily blinded her. She swung her racket and missed, and the shuttle landed close to her left eye. When she dropped the racket and covered her eye with her hand, Brian ran to her side.

"Are you all right?" he asked.

He lightly grasped her hand and moved it away, and he was relieved when he saw a dark red mark on her left cheek.

"That was close. It barely missed your eye."

One of the elders from the church let out a loud whistle at that time, inviting everyone to gather around the tables for second helpings before they put the food away, and the teenagers on the field instantly took off, but Brian and Sarah remained where they were.

Brian gently caressed the mark on her cheek. "Does that hurt?"

He expected her to shy away from his touch, but instead she covered his hand with hers and pressed it more firmly against her cheek. "*Neh,*" she murmured.

Brian felt caught between a rock and a hard place. He knew the right thing to do would be to remove his hand, but that was the last thing he wanted to do. It felt wonderful touching her, and even though he knew her heart belonged to someone else, he decided to enjoy the moment while it lasted.

She parted her lips and Brian swallowed hard. He could feel her warm breath on his skin, which made his pulse quicken, and her mesmerizing blue eyes held him still and wouldn't let go. He wanted to kiss her – *needed* to kiss her – more than he needed the air to breathe.

"Sarah, are you sure you're all right? You looked upset before the game started..."

She instantly released his hand and backed away before he finished his sentence. Her eyes filled with tears, and Brian felt like kicking himself – again. Why, oh why, did he have such a terrible knack for saying the wrong thing at the wrong time?

"I'm fine," she replied. "We should go."

He tried to stop her from leaving, but she was too quick. Before he knew it, she'd turned on her heel and was walking briskly toward the church, and he had no other choice but to follow. Once they made it back among the congregation, she melded into the crowd and disappeared from his sight.

Meredith Miller sidled up next to him and tried to get his attention, but she was the last person he cared to speak to. When she winked at him and tried to hook her arm through his, he stepped away and joined his parents, who were still deep in conversation with their neighbors.

"Everything all right, son?" his *daed* asked.

He gave him a weak nod before searching the crowd once again for Sarah, but she was nowhere to be found.

* * * *

"You look like you have the weight of the world on your shoulders."

Startled, Sarah jumped before turning in the direction of the deep male voice, nearly dropping the letter she'd spent all morning trying to finish. Brian stood a few feet behind her, with a sly grin on his face and his hands stuffed inside the front pockets of his trousers.

"I'm sorry. I didn't mean to frighten you."

Sarah took a couple of breaths to try and soothe her pounding heart. She laughed softly once she realized how ridiculous she must have looked to him and any other passersby she may have missed while lost in thought. She had no idea how long she'd been standing by her mailbox, silently contemplating whether or not the letter in her hand should be sent or tossed into a trash can.

"It's okay," she replied. "If you hadn't come by, there's no telling how long I would've stood here, looking like some kind of bump on a log."

Brian chuckled as he drew closer. "Are you all right?"

Sarah looked into his light brown eyes and saw the concern written as clear as day on his handsome face. She contemplated telling him what was weighing so heavily on her mind, but she didn't want to burden him – or anyone – with her problems. Since her arrival in Lancaster, everyone had treated her with such kindness and her aunt Hope did everything possible to make her feel comfortable in her new home. Even Brian took time out of his busy week to stop by and check on her. It was quite endearing and so complaining about her troubles didn't feel like the right way to repay them for their generosity.

"I tell you what," Brian said. "Come with me for a few minutes, and maybe by the time we return you'll be able to decide whether or not to mail that letter."

Sarah frowned, realizing he must have seen the letter was addressed to Abraham, which was embarrassing, and her cheeks reddened as she slipped the envelope inside a pocket of her apron. If he wondered what her apprehension was about, he didn't mention it, and for that she was grateful.

"Where were you going?" she asked.

Brian gestured for her to walk with him, and as she fell in step beside him, she noticed they were heading in the direction of his house. She honestly didn't feel like visiting with his mother and Bishop Eli, but she didn't object either. It was obvious he could tell something was wrong, and he was just trying to be kind, so Sarah smiled and went along with whatever he had in mind.

"I need to check on my property," he announced.

Sarah furrowed a brow, not recalling Brian or anyone else mentioning they had more property in another location. Several yards past his house, she discovered a well-traveled dirt road to the left that pierced through a dense grove of oak trees.

"*Your* property or your parents?"

Brian rolled his eyes heavenward.

"It's mine. I don't plan on living with my parents forever, Sarah. I know most people choose to live with theirs until they get married, but I have bigger goals I want to accomplish and one of those is living in my own house – sooner rather than later."

Sarah smiled. She admired his tenacity and was quite impressed he'd planned so far ahead, unlike most of her friends, who were obsessed over courting and marriage and little else. She and Brian walked just a few feet when the road opened to a wide clearing that was surrounded by tall, majestic oaks and pine trees. On the far-right side of the property was a small pond, and directly in front of them was the shell of what she guessed was Brian's house.

The boards for the foundation, walls, and roof were in place, and as they drew closer, she could more easily distinguish the floor plan, which included two small bedrooms, a kitchen, a bathroom, and a dining room. While they walked from room to room, Brian's eyes lit up with excitement as he described his plans for each one, and she couldn't help but smile over his enthusiasm.

Brian couldn't have chosen a more stunning setting to build a house, and as she leaned against one of the boards and gazed upon the expansive property, she had to admit she felt a little envious.

"It's beautiful, Brian. I'm so happy for you."

She meant it too. Anyone who spent most of their teenage years saving up money to build a house deserved praise.

"*Denki*. I'm glad you like it. Have you and Abraham started talking house plans yet?"

Her spine stiffened at the mention of his name, and she fervently shook her head before looking the opposite way so Brian wouldn't see her eyes swell with tears. "Abraham hasn't breathed a word about a wedding – much less talked about building a house."

She could sense Brian moving closer, but she didn't turn around. When he placed a hand against the small of her back, the warmth of his touch made her tremble.

"Sarah, I'm so sorry. Sometimes I don't know when to keep my big mouth shut."

His comment brought a smile to her face, and she hastily wiped her eyes before trusting herself to look at him.

"It's all right – really. I'm sorry I got defensive, but...I don't see a future involving me and Abraham walking down the aisle together."

He looked genuinely surprised, and he didn't say a word for a long time.

"Sarah, I know we haven't known each other long, but I hope you know you can talk to me about anything. If I don't have the answers, I'm sure my *daed* would be more than happy to counsel you."

Again, Sarah shook her head. She greatly admired Bishop Eli, but the thought of talking to a member of the clergy about something so intimate and personal made her uncomfortable.

Sarah sat down and dangled her legs over the wooden foundation that would soon be Brian's front porch and he sat down beside her. They were so close she could hear his slow, even breaths, which helped to settle her frazzled mind.

"I appreciate your concern, Brian. To be honest with you, I don't know what the future holds for me and Abraham. I used to think we would spend the rest of our lives together, but I received a letter from him last week and now he feels that the distance between us is too much of a hurdle to overcome."

Brian squinted.

"If he truly loves you, then something as trivial as the miles from Dayton to Lancaster shouldn't cause a problem. He could always move here. There's plenty of jobs to be found."

She wasn't sure if the disdain she detected in his voice was real or just something she imagined, but she tried not to make much of it.

Sarah sighed.

"I think there's more to it than just the distance," she admitted. "My parents used to pick on me all the time that he was nothing but a 'charmer', but I guess I chose to ignore it. He's had girls fawning over him since we were children, and I could sense in his letter that he's feeling...neglected."

The thought of Ann Wilkes, Samantha King, and the other single women back home in Dayton chasing after Abraham during her absence made her sick to her stomach.

"I'm guessing by the way you hesitated mailing your letter that you had something very important to say to him."

Sarah smoothed a hand over the pocket of her apron where the envelope was safely tucked away.

"I told him I understood but that I felt like we could work through a long-distance relationship."

Brian didn't say anything, but she didn't miss the not-so subtle shake of his head or the way he clenched his jaw.

"What's wrong?" she asked.

He slid off the platform and walked a couple of feet before turning around to face her with his arms crossed over his chest.

"I promise I'm not trying to make you angry, Sarah, but it sounds like you're groveling."

She was taken aback by his reply, and at first, she didn't know how to respond and, yes, there was a small hint of anger that began to swell inside her chest.

"Sarah, just please hear me out. You just said that Brian was used to women chasing after him, and you were here only a couple of weeks before he decided to write and tell you that the distance was too much for him. From a man's viewpoint, it sounds like he just wants an easy way out so he can date other women. If he truly loved you, he would find a way to make this work."

She knew he had a valid point, but it still stung, nonetheless. True, her and Abraham's relationship was fairly new, and perhaps she *was* clinging too desperately to it because she was afraid of being alone.

"I apologize, Sarah," he said, softly. "Here I go running my mouth again when I should just mind my own business."

Sarah felt pulled in so many different directions, she didn't know whether to be angry at him or thank him for being so blunt.

"I should go. My aunt Hope is probably wondering where I am."

Brian reached for her, but she moved away from his grasp.

"Sarah, please..."

She shook her head and walked away before he could say anything else. She didn't want to hear another word. All she wanted – and needed – was the peace and quiet necessary to sort through her own thoughts.

* * * *

The minutes were passing by far too slowly for Brian's liking. As he watched another horde of Lancaster inhabitants invade one of the small dessert booths at their annual festival the following weekend, he was glad all he had to do was help people load furniture into their vehicles. As luck would have it, he'd never excelled at cooking.

The festival was held every year to help raise money for the Lancaster Volunteer Fire Department, and it was always a huge success. By the amount of cakes, pies, furniture, quilts, and other goods he'd seen flying off the tables, *Gott* was richly blessing this year's festivities too.

Brian stole a glance at Sarah's booth, where she and Miss Hope were busy selling their homemade jellies and jams, and his insides twisted into one big painful knot. They hadn't spoken since their awkward conversation on his homestead about her relationship with Abraham, and he was afraid he may have permanently ruined their friendship.

Brian groaned out loud as he looked down at his feet and angrily kicked some stones out of his path. Whatever spark he'd felt between the two of them – if it could even be called that – was long gone, and he was so clueless when it came to women, he had no idea how to make it right. Perhaps one day she'd be able to forgive him for sticking his foot in his mouth.

"Looks like you could use a friend."

Brian was almost afraid to look up. He knew that voice all too well, and it wasn't one he welcomed. Actually, after the way his week had gone, it was the last voice he needed to hear at the moment.

"*Hallo*, Meredith."

He was sure he sounded tired and unpleasant, but he knew where this conversation was headed before it even started, and he wanted to nip it in the bud as quickly as possible. He wasn't interested in Meredith, and he wasn't going to string her along because it wouldn't be right.

"I baked one of my famous strawberry cakes just for you, and it's stashed away under the table in my booth, so I'll be looking for you when this festival is over."

Brian groaned. He'd never met someone as aggressive as Meredith, and it was extremely annoying. He'd tried several times to let her down gently, but apparently, that wasn't working. He didn't want to be mean, but how else could he get his point across?

"Meredith, I appreciate your thoughtfulness. Really, I do," he began, hesitantly. "But there's no way..."

"There you are!"

He stopped abruptly at the sweet sound of Sarah's voice, and before he had to time to comprehend what was happening, she was by his side and hooking her arm through his before planting a kiss on his cheek.

"I've been looking all over for you," she continued. "You promised me lunch, and I'm here to collect."

Meredith's jaw slacked, but it didn't take long for her to compose herself, and when she stood up straight and thrust out her chin, Brian braced himself for the worst. Sarah, however, looked like she could burst out laughing any minute.

"I see," Meredith stated. "Well, I won't keep you waiting. Goodbye Brian."

When she turned sharply on her heel and walked away, he felt both relieved and a tad bit remorseful. It wasn't how he planned to let her down easy, but it did work, even if it was all a ruse.

"What was that about?" he asked, trying to contain his laughter.

Sarah smiled as she tugged on his arm and pulled him in the opposite direction.

"I saw you from my booth and the look on your face...it resembled a deer caught in the headlights, and I thought you needed saving."

Brian couldn't help himself, and when he burst out laughing, Sarah did too.

"Well, you were right, so...*denki.*"

She nodded, and they walked in silence for a few minutes, taking in the sights and trying to weave their way through the horde of people pushing past them. He hoped this meant she'd forgiven him, but he still held his breath.

"I guess I owe you some lunch then," he said. "It's the least I can do for you coming to my rescue."

Sarah took his hand and when she laced her fingers through his, the heat that coursed through his veins caught him off guard and nearly sent him tumbling to the ground. Her skin was soft and warm, and when she pulled him away from the crowd to an empty, secluded spot behind one of the booths, it felt as if his heart might pound right out of his chest.

"Can I say something first?" she asked. "I've been thinking a lot about what you said the other day, and you were right."

Brian gave her a quizzical look.

"Abraham called a couple of days ago, and his intentions were very clear. He was prying me for answers – asking if I'd given any thought to what he wrote in his letter and really just trying to make me agree so his conscious would be clear and he could start dating other people – if he hasn't already."

Sarah rolled her eyes heavenward.

"It was pathetic and made me realize he's not worth pining after. Honestly, no one who acts in such a way is worth that, and I respect myself too much to even consider it. So...we broke up."

He was surprised when she didn't sound or act upset over it in the least bit, and she quickly changed the subject, as if talking about it left a bad taste in her mouth. Seeing her beautiful smile and hearing the positive, happy tone of her voice made his spirits soar. Before he knew it, he was sweeping her off her feet and twirling her around in his arms, and Sarah was laughing out loud by the time he planted her feet back on the ground.

"What was that for?" she asked.

Brian looked up at the blue sky and grinned from ear to ear, while keeping his hands firmly on her waist.

"I'm just happy for you, Sarah. I haven't seen you smile this much since you moved here, and you sound so much more content than the day I picked you up from the bus terminal."

She placed her hands on his shoulders and looked up at him with the most loving expression, he thought for certain his heart would burst.

"I guess I haven't really thought much about it, but you're right. Don't get me wrong – I miss my brothers and sisters more than ever, but it does give me peace knowing they're happy and that someone is taking such good care of them. I may not get to see them as often as I'd like to, but we're family and nothing will ever change that. As far as Abraham is concerned, I suppose I was blinded by his charm. Thank you for helping me see the truth."

When she stood on her tiptoes and kissed his cheek, Brian pulled her close to his body to keep her from moving away from him too quickly. Their lips were so close he could feel her warm breath dance across his skin, and he physically ached to kiss her, but he also didn't want to frighten her by moving too fast. Before he could decide what to do, Sarah stood on her tiptoes again and kissed him gently on the lips. It was a brief kiss, but the effect it had on him was overwhelming, and he held her tighter to keep his legs from shaking.

"To new beginnings," she whispered, before kissing him again.

Brian smiled as he tucked a strand of her hair behind her left ear before delicately tracing her jawline with his fingertips. "To new beginnings."

LOVINA'S DAED

MARY DOWNES

"What is that noise?" Lovina asked, looking up at the door.

The rattling sound had persisted all the way through church service, and even when two of the boys had moved a chair to lean against the door, the door had rattled and buzzed with every gust of wind.

"Maybe," Sadie said, barely glancing at the door. "What were you saying?"

"I was asking if you'd noticed anything about my *daed*," said Lovina. "If you thought anything had... changed."

The door rattled again. Lovina reached out and pressed lightly against the latch, to feel whether or not it was responsible for the sound, but there was no change. She pressed harder.

"What are you doing?" asked Sadie.

"I have an idea... so did you notice anything?"

"I think you'd be more likely to notice than me," Sadie pointed out. "What sort of thing are you talking about?"

"Just sort of... the things he's saying, I guess."

Lovina looked back up at the door, and tried pressing against the hinges. Still nothing.

"I know you wouldn't notice so much as me, but he's been up at your place every spare moment these past two weeks. I've only seen him for the odd meal here or there. I thought maybe you might have picked up on something."

"Oh. Well, he's not been in the house," said Sadie. "He and my *daed* and the boys have been working on the cottage, and that's all the way down the end of the property."

"Right, of course."

The cottage on Sadie's family's farm had previously only ever been rented out to seasonal laborers, and had been kept in a rough, unfinished state. But it had recently been let to a newcomer to the community – a widow. Sadie's mother had insisted that the cottage be made suitable for a lady occupant.

The door was still rattling. Lovina tried its corners. Bottom left, top left, top right – *there* it was. As she pushed against the corner of the door, the rattling stopped. She let go, and it started again.

"I was just wondering if anything had happened," continued Lovina. She grabbed a piece of paper from the basket of kindling scraps by the door and started folding it up. "He's been talking about *mamme*."

"Really?" Sadie looked surprised.

"I know. The first time in years."

"Just..." Sadie hesitated delicately. "Just your *mamme*? Not..."

"Not Mary, no."

John rarely spoke of his dead wife – but he never, never spoke of Mary.

Lovina reached up and wedged the folded piece of paper into the gap between the corner of the door and its frame. The noise stopped.

"Good job," said Sadie, looking up at the door.

"Girls!" called Sadie's mother, Elsa, from inside the kitchen. "Come on, the first load of dishes need doing."

"Coming, *mamme*," called Sadie. She turned back to Lovina. "Tell you what. I'll keep an eye out for any time I see your *daed* this week."

"But they're done with the cottage, aren't they?" Now it was Lovina's turn to be surprised. "I thought – the widow, what's her name?"

"Miriam. Miriam – uh, Stolzfus."

"I thought she had moved in already."

"She has, three days ago," affirmed Sadie. "They were just going to finish whitewashing the outside, but I heard your *daed* tell mine that the roof needed work as well. He said he'd be coming over next week to see to it."

Lovina shook her head as they made their way into the kitchen. Why hadn't he said anything to her about this?

***

"That's her?"

Sadie nodded, helping herself to potatoes.

"She's beautiful."

The widow, standing and speaking to Sadie's mother and father across the yard, was truly lovely. She was tall, two inches taller than Lovina. Her skin looked clear and free of lines, her hair was smooth and dark, her features finely set.

Lovina was not sure why she was surprised. Perhaps it was because all the widows she had known in her life had been over the age of sixty.

As she watched, Lovina saw her father walk over to the little group.

It was odd, Lovina thought, the way he walked. She was used to him walking with his head downcast – just a little, not so as anyone would really notice. Not unless they were looking. Not unless they had known him as he had been before.

Maybe it was all that time he had spent with Sadie's father and her brothers recently, Lovina thought. For the past three years, John had kept to himself as much as possible, only joining in with group events when it was something that the entire community was expected at, like the occasional barn raising.

Lovina had been the one to suggest he go over and help set up the new cottage, lending his construction skills. She had thought it would be good for him to get out of the house, though she had almost not expected him to agree.

Socializing was clearly good for him. She watched him talking, now, and he looked happy. He almost never looked happy. He had obviously rekindled his friendship with Sadie's parents, and he was even talking to the widow, whom he must have met when she moved into the cottage.

Yes, thought Lovina. It was good that he would be returning the following week to continue to work on the cottage, even if it did mean that she would be spending more time alone.

Later, Lovina was given an opportunity to meet the widow herself.

She had kept busy, helping with the serving, and had not really spoken to anyone. Then, during the normal time of socializing afterward, she had continued to catch up with Sadie, whom she had not seen much of in the past few weeks as she had also been helping prepare the cottage.

"It seems like you've all been working non stop on that place," Lovina commented to Sadie as they stood together in the shade of an oak tree at the side of the yard.

They had finished helping to clean, and were now watching as the tables and chairs were packed back into their long wagon.

"We only had the two weeks," said Sadie. "That was when we got her Miriam's letter asking if she could rent the place."

"You mean she only took the place at two weeks notice? That seems odd."

Sadie shrugged. "She'd been living with her brother since her husband died. Then he decided to get married, and she wanted to give his new wife the run of the house without worrying about her."

"Hmm," said Lovina. "I wonder if that means she didn't get on with the brother's wife. Do you think?"

Perhaps the new wife was unpleasant, or controlling. Or maybe Miriam herself was not that easy to get on with...

"Who knows," said Sadie, distracted by the sight of her seven-year-old brother darting in amongst the men who were lifting the heavy wooden folding tables. He knocked against one of the men, who almost lost his grip on the end he was carrying.

"Andrew!" Sadie called out. "Careful!"

"*Mamme* said I could help," Andrew called back, attempting to grasp the side of a table that was being lifted.

"He's going to hurt himself," said Sadie worriedly, waving over at her mother.

Elsa, coming out if the kitchen, immediately sized up the situation and beckoned Andrew over to her.

"You said I could help," he began, sounding put out.

"Of course," said his mother. "But I have a more important job for you. Can you be very strong, and help me carry all of the dishwashing tubs down into the cellar?"

Andrew, puffing himself up with importance, hurried into the kitchen.

Lovina and Sadie laughed.

"I always preferred that method myself," came a voice to their left.

Turning, Lovina saw the widow. Miriam. She was looking over at Elsa and nodding in approval.

"Subtlety," she said.

"It sure is," said Sadie. "Miriam, this is Lovina Fisher, my best friend. Lovina, Mrs. Miriam Stolzfus."

"Nice to meet you," Lovina said automatically.

Now that she had the chance to see Miriam up close, she realized that she was not quite that young. There were a few lines around her eyes and mouth; her hair, though mostly dark, was shot through with a silvery gray. She was still beautiful, though.

"Oh, Lovina," said Miriam, smiling. "Your father has mentioned you."

Lovina blinked. Her father had mentioned her?

"Really?" she said.

"Yes. It was good to hear how great a help you've been to him after your family's losses." Miriam smiled sadly. "I wish I could have had such support. It's really wonderful."

Miriam's words sank in slowly. There was a brief pause, in which Lovina guessed she should say something – but she could not make a sound.

After a moment, Sadie stepped in. "Yes, Lovina and her *daed* are very close," she said.

Miriam nodded, still holding her soft, sad smile in place, before moving on.

Lovina stared after her as she moved away.

Her father had been talking about her to this woman? And not only that – not only that – he had spoken of their losses. *Losses,* plural. Meaning that he had not only talked of his wife's death with someone who was almost a complete stranger, when he barely even talked to Lovina about it, but he had also spoken of Mary.

Mary, whose name had not passed in their conversation since her funeral four years ago. Who had not even been mentioned by Lovina's *mamme* on her deathbed.

What is going on? wondered Lovina, though she did not speak the question aloud. Some small part of her realized that she already knew the answer.

Later still, when she and John were driving home, Lovina still would not let herself answer the question. Even when she noticed, again, how her father was looking up at the sky, the way she remembered him doing when she was little, and he would point out cloud shapes to her and Mary.

Not even when he asked her, in a falsely casual manner, whether she had met the newcomer.

"She's very nice," said Lovina, trying to ignore the way her chest suddenly felt cold, as though she were slowly filling with iced water.

***

"He didn't *tell* you?"

Sadie seemed incredulous. Lovina supposed that with her big, loud family, always in each others' pockets, the idea of keeping any kind of secret was unthinkable.

"No," she said, opening the door of the gas powered refrigerator and pulling out two jugs of cold tea. "You're sure you saw them together?"

Not that Lovina had needed a confirmation. Her father had continued to find things "wrong" with the widow's cottage, going back week after week for the past month.

"Two days ago," affirmed Sadie, shutting the refrigerator door. "Walking together at sunset, down by the river."

"I see." Lovina placed the jugs on the table and started arranging the plates of cookies. "Well, he probably didn't want to say anything unless he thought – "

It might lead to marriage.

"Unless he thought something could happen," she said.

"In case he upset you?" asked Sadie.

"Maybe," said Lovina. She listened carefully to the women talking outside.

A group had come over to help her with her canning, the way they did every year. This year, the newcomer had been invited along as well; of course she had, it would have been strange otherwise. Lovina had been trying not to speak directly to Miriam, just in case she gave something away. The last thing she needed was for the women to come in and catch her and Sadie talking about this.

"*Are* you upset?" pressed Sadie.

"No…" said Lovina slowly. "Not that he might want to get married. That's to be expected."

Though she had not expected it. Not from the man who had spent the last three years staring at the floor, and talking only to her.

"I'm just not sure about *her*."

"Miriam? What's wrong with her?" asked Sadie.

"I don't know. I'm not sure I trust her. We don't know anything about her, really."

"What's to know?" said Sadie, surveying the finished table. "Her husband passed away, she lived with her brother, then he got married and she moved out here."

"But where did she move from?" asked Lovina. "Who's this brother she decided to leave behind so suddenly? And why did she move at all – could she really not stand sharing a house with another woman? Why start from scratch? Why cut yourself off from all your friends and family, and live among strangers?"

"She moved from Green River in Indiana," said Sadie matter-of-factly. "And her brother's name is Jay. As to why she moved, you could always ask her."

"What makes you think she'd tell me the truth?" asked Lovina.

Sadie stared at her. "When did you become so skeptical?" she asked.

They were interrupted by one of the women – an older woman named Barbara, who was not known for her patience, putting her head through the kitchen door and asking if they were ready.

"Ready," said Lovina. "Come on in for refreshments!"

She ignored Sadie, who was still looking at her as though expecting an answer. What could she say? She knew that her emotions might well be affecting her judgment, but she could swear there was something about Miriam that was... off.

When the women entered and sat, Lovina was greatly displeased to find that Miriam took the seat right next to hers.

"Thank you again, everyone, for coming over," she said, hoping to keep the conversation general by addressing the table at large, rather than having to speak directly to her neighbor.

There was a general chorus of "of course, no trouble, you'd do the same for us."

"Lovina is a wonderful housekeeper," said Barbara, leaning over to Miriam.

"I can see that," smiled Miriam, glancing around the spotless kitchen.

"Been taking care of it all herself since she was fourteen, isn't that right, Lovina?"

Lovina looked down at her glass of tea.

"That's wonderful," said Miriam.

No it isn't, Lovina wanted to shout. How could Miriam of all people not understand what that meant?

Lovina's domain over the kitchen had been bestowed when her mother had fallen ill. Or, no, even before that; after Mary had died, *mamme* had struggled to manage her work. With no other siblings, Lovina had taken on as much as she could to save her mother trouble.

She had assumed, at the time, that her mother would take the reigns back as soon as she was able. But the diagnosis had come first.

The conversation returned to safer waters for a while, as everyone started talking about all the canning they needed to get done before the end of summer. Miriam was very interested to hear that there would be a market in early fall – she was having to buy everything at the moment, as her vegetable garden would not be ready for any sort of harvest this year.

"Will you be selling any of today's cherries?" she asked Lovina.

Lovina simply nodded, allowing the conversation to pass by her.

"Her sour cherries are even better," said someone down the table. "We did those a month ago."

"My husband can't get enough of sour cherry pie," said someone else. "I think he'd live on it if he were able."

"I always preferred the sour cherries to the sweet myself," said Miriam, smiling. "My husband was the one with the sweet tooth. One of the few things we ever disagreed on."

There were sympathetic nods up and down the table.

"Loss is a hard thing to bear," was Barbara's brilliant and insightful comment, as she looked at Miriam and then at Lovina.

Miriam nodded, and glanced at Lovina. Lovina flushed. The widow clearly thought they were having some kind of moment. She knew they she should say something, but she just couldn't bring herself to. What was it about Miriam that kept leaving her tongue-tied?

As the conversation finally moved on once more, Lovina did her best to avoid Sadie's still-questioning gaze; Sadie would have considered that moment a chance to open up to Miriam. Lovina did not know how to explain to her friend how necessary it was to hide her heart. She and John had both locked theirs away years ago.

It had been hard enough dealing with the suddenness of Mary's death. Her death was the first tragedy Lovina had ever experienced, and she was completely unprepared. She had never known anyone who had died before, and had no context for the sudden, shattering blow and the gaping hole it left behind.

They had barely begun to deal with it when *mamme* had become ill. At that point, Lovina accepted every day as a continuation of some bad dream. After the diagnosis, the cancer had swept in with speed and without mercy, leaving them breathless and stunned when *mamme* had passed not three months after that first trip to the doctor.

She and John had dealt with their grief separately, as the idea of holding someone else's feelings as well as their own had seemed impossibly overwhelming. They had wrapped themselves up, and hidden away.

And now John was re-emerging. And Lovina had been left behind.

Was that why she was feeling this way? Maybe it was nothing to do with Miriam.

Maybe she was being selfish.

I should try, thought Lovina. *If I try to get to know her, reach out a little... at least if I learn more about her, then I can know for sure if there's anything to worry about, or if it's just me.*

Yes, that's an idea.

And so, as the canning party broke up later that afternoon and everyone started heading home, Lovina quickly ran down to the cellar and grabbed a jar of her sour cherries.

Running back upstairs, she spotted Sadie and Miriam about to leave, and waved at them to wait. Without giving herself time to hesitate, she walked over, pretending that she could not see Sadie looking worried.

"These are for you," she said, to Miriam, proffering the jar. "Sour cherries, to get your winter stock started."

Miriam took it, looking delighted. "That's so sweet of you," she said. "I really do love these in a pie."

"They're my favorites, too," Lovina said, feeling as though she was making a great concession in sharing personal information with Miriam.

"I'll try to make these last," Miriam said, still smiling. "They always got eaten up so quickly at home. This was really very nice of you, Lovina. If I stay long enough at the cottage, I'll hopefully have a harvest to pay you back with."

And then she and Sadie left, and Sadie looked behind her as she walked, communicating her approval at the effort Lovina had made. And Lovina stared after them.

What did she just say?

She went though it again in her head. Slowly, so as to be sure she was not making a mistake.

No, I heard right, she thought.

But what does that mean?

***

"*Daed?*"

"Hmm?" John looked over at his daughter. "What is it?"

Lovina looked down at her lap and nervously twitched the apron she was mending. She had brought it out to the porch, joining her father as he sat. But she had not been able to make a single stitch as she had thought about how to speak with him.

He was sitting to the side, looking out at the view taking in the sunset. It was certainly worth looking at, as the bright yellow clouds slowly singed themselves into red and the corn fields' gold deepened as though they were catching fire.

Lovina could not remember the last time she had seen John look so at peace.

And she had to break it.

"Ah – well, *daed*, you know Miriam – "

As she had feared, John immediately tensed.

"What about her?" he asked.

Well, what about her, Lovina thought, hesitating.

This was the problem; she did not have anything set in stone that she could tell her father. No evidence. Wouldn't he assume, as Sadie had, that Lovina was simply angry at the idea of her mother being replaced? He might think that she was upset he had kept his courtship of Miriam a secret from her.

John looked guilty already. Flustered.

Lovina wondered when she had last seen so many emotions play out across his face.

Not when *mamme* died. He had already shut himself away by then. For just a moment, Lovina did feel angry, really angry, that her father had withdrawn from his wife, and her, his daughter, and that he had needed some beautiful stranger to come and wake him from his slumber. She wanted to lash out and hurt him so that he would go back into hiding where he belonged, where she still was.

But no. She could not hold such dark thoughts in her heart. She loved her father. She knew he loved her, and that he may well love Miriam.

How could she do this to him?

And what if she was wrong?

A memory rose, unbidden. The last time Lovina had seen her father become emotional – really, truly, emotional, allowing himself to be so.

The day of Mary's death. She had heard him, from where he had been working with *mamme* in the kitchen. He had been screaming. *No, no, no.*

Lovina had rushed outside, pausing in the yard for just a moment to listen for where the sound was coming from. The barn, she had realized, and had begun to run towards it, calling out to John, asking what had happened. *I'm coming, daed.*

He had met her at the doorway of the barn. Stopped her, arms outstretched, pushing backwards and trying to shield her from getting a better look at the sight she had just managed to glimpse: a crumpled figure, lying awkwardly beneath the hole to the hay loft, the thin layer of straw on the ground around it stained dark.

There's been an accident, he had said. *Go up and tell your mamme, I'm right behind.* He had waited to tell her the truth. Protected her. She would do the same for him.

"I gave her some of our cherries," said Lovina. She picked up her needle and began working on the apron, keeping her gaze fixed downward as carefully as though she had never mended anything in her life before.

"That was nice of you," said John cautiously.

What a fine family we are, Lovina thought, her heart aching. *Sitting here and deceiving each other.*

"She was so pleased with them, I wished I'd given her a second jar," she continued. "I thought maybe if you were going back to work on the cottage, you might take one over?"

John nodded, as though it did not really matter one way or the other. "Sure," he said.

Lovina did not speak again, her eyes on her mending and her mind on what she would have to do.

She had an idea.

***

"How much longer do you think you'll be?"

Lovina looked up from her search.

"Sorry, Tom," she said. "I'm not sure... hopefully not long."

She looked over at Sadie, who was leaning against the wall next to a display of postcards with her eyes closed.

"Can't you lend a hand?" she called over.

"First of all," said Sadie, holding up one finger without opening her eyes, "I am still feeling sick from that car ride. I don't know how you spend all day in that thing, Tom."

"You get used to it," said Tom, rolling his eyes. It was a gesture that seemed oddly young for a man in his sixties.

Sadie held up another finger. "And second, I think what you're doing is insane, and I do not want to help you."

"Then why did you come?" asked Lovina, going back to looking through the bookshelves.

"Because whenever you utter the words 'I have an idea' I know that whatever follows is unavoidable," said Sadie. "All I can do is follow and make sure you don't do anything too crazy."

"She's got a point," said Tom.

"Why don't you get a cup of coffee, Tom?" suggested Lovina, pretending she had not heard either of them. "I'll pay."

"Nah," said Tom. "I've got a thermos in the car. Besides, the fare out here and back's going to cost you enough as it is... why don't I help you look? Which one is it again?"

"Green River," said Lovina. "Indiana."

Tom joined her at the bookshelf and started sorting through the directories.

Lovina was grateful that she knew Tom so well; she couldn't imagine most drivers would be willing to do this. Tom had taken the family up to the hospital and back several times during *mamme's* illness, and had become friendly with all of them. When he learned how serious the situation really was, he had given the family his personal number and told them to call any time they needed a ride. His mother had passed away from cancer too, he had said.

Tom had been the one to take them on that last trip to see *mamme*, and had bought Lovina a hot chocolate to drink on the way home, telling her sweetness was good for shock. Lovina had not seen him since then, as she had never needed a car, but he had remembered her as soon as she had called early this morning.

He had not even blinked when she had explained why she needed to be driven to the "Amish Gift Shoppe" over an hour away in Willow Grove.

Although he had pointed out that he had never had a request from an Amish person to go to the tourist shop unless they had a job there or were selling something. This was true enough – most of the people that Lovina knew tolerated these gift shops as a chance to sell crafts and cookery, but otherwise found them annoying. Lovina had only ever been in here once before, to arrange the sale of some of the crafts and canned goods left over from the yearly market.

She remembered seeing the assortment of directories and wondering why on earth they were selling such things in a gift shop. As though tourists had any right to peruse those pages and learn the names and ages of those who lived in the communities – for which the directories had actually been printed.

But now, she was grateful. Because not only did the shop sell directories, it boasted "directories of every Amish community in a thousand square miles (three for the price of two)". Which was exactly what she needed.

And, hopefully – *yes*. There it was.

"Got it," said Lovina. "Green River."

Lovina wanted to start looking through the booklet immediately, but the teen at the counter had been giving the group strange looks for the past few minutes. She would have to wait until she got home.

"So this is the clue you needed?" asked Tom, leaning against the counter as Lovina paid for the booklet. "To find out if this widow is lying?"

"I guess. I mean, I don't *want* her to be lying. I just... need to check. Could I have a bag for this?"

The teen grunted and disappeared into a stock room behind the counter.

"Fair enough," said Tom. "And how will the book help, if I can ask?"

"It lists the families that live in the community," explained Lovina. "Names, ages, and so on. Marriages and children."

"So you – what, you think she's lying about being married?"

"I think..." Lovina looked back down at the book. "I think she might have children."

Lovina could see Sadie shaking her head out of the corner of her eye. Sadie had already stated her opinion, multiple times, that Lovina was just looking for something to be wrong. That she wanted a reason for Miriam to be unsuitable.

But Lovina knew, she just *knew* that she was on to something.

And if Miriam did have children – if Lovina was right – then she had lied about it. And she had left them – where? And why? And who could tell, if she was lying about having children, then she might well still be married after all. She could have abandoned her family and come here, to start a new life. With John Fisher.

But Lovina would find out.

"Really," said Tom. "How'd you figure?"

"It was a few comments," said Lovina. "About children, and..." she hesitated. "And, well, cherries."

"Cherries," repeated Tom dubiously.

"I know how it sounds," said Lovina.

"And yet we're still here," came Sadie's voice from behind them.

Lovina shook her head and lapsed into silence and the teen reappeared with a brown paper bag for the booklet and a confused expression. Blushing, Lovina realized that their voices had probably carried into the stockroom.

When they reached home, Lovina had Tom drop her and Sadie off in a side road so they could walk home without being spotted. She nodded when he told her to say hi to her dad from him, although she knew that she could not say anything to her father about seeing Tom without having to explain what she had needed a car for.

Lovina and Sadie parted ways at the end of Lovina's lane.

"You didn't have to come, today," said Lovina. "But thank you all the same."

Sadie's face creased with sadness. "Oh, Lovina," she said, enveloping her friend in a hug. "I hope you're wrong, I really do."

"So do I," said Lovina, hoping fervently that she was telling the truth.

As soon as she reached the house, she settled herself at the kitchen table, poured a glass of water, took the booklet out of its bag, and began to leaf through it.

She almost wished, afterward, that it had taken her longer. Every moment before she knew the truth, she could keep herself in the space between knowing and unknowing. She did not have to face the part of herself that wanted Miriam to be guilty.

But the Plain community at Green River, Indiana, was not a large one, and the directory did not take long to read, so it only took a few minutes for Lovina to make her way through the entire thing without once reading the name "Miriam Stolzfus."

There was a Miriam Hoder, and a Miriam Mast. No Miriam Stolzfus.

Lovina checked the pages again, telling herself that she might have missed the name, all the while knowing that she had not missed it, and feeling a sickly rush of vindication, knowing that she had been right. Miriam had been lying.

And she, Lovina, was... happy about this? She did not want to be happy about this.

Turning back to her task, Lovina wondered whether Miriam might not have gone back to her maiden name, although that would be very unusual.

Lovina soon found one family named Stolzfus, but it was an elderly couple with two sons who had married an Esther and a Grace, and both new couples were in their early twenties.

She also looked for a Jay, Stolzfus or otherwise, but either Miriam had lied to Sadie about her brother's name or it was a nickname.

Would Miriam have even kept her first name? Lovina wondered. Or even told the truth about where she was from in the first place?

But she would probably have given something away if she was going by a false first name, like forgetting to answer when people addressed her directly. Miriam, Lovina knew now, was not very good at lying

It had been the cherries that had done it. Miriam had told Lovina that she always had requests for sour cherries at home. But before, she had told everyone that her husband did not like them. So who was making the requests?

It had not been quite enough by itself, but then Lovina had remembered the day she had met Miriam. The way she had looked at Sadie's mother with little Andrew, saying that she liked a similar approach herself. The way she had said it had made it sound, Lovina thought, as though she herself had children.

And now this.

Lovina went back to the two Miriams she had found. Which would it be? They were both married – the directory had been printed two years ago, and would not have recorded the death of Miriam's husband which, according to Sadie, had occurred only one year ago. Unless that was also a lie.

So. Miriam Mast had a young daughter, and a twelve year old son. She herself was in her early thirties. Two young to be the Miriam Lovina knew, surely? *Although some people do go gray early...*

But then she looked at Miriam Hoder. Forty years old, married to David Hoder, with three children. Sister of... James Lapp.

"*Jay,*" whispered Lovina.

This was her. This was Miriam.

Three children... David Jr., fifteen years old, Isaac, eleven, and Peter, six.

She did have children.

And... she had left them behind?

Why?

"Why would she leave you?" Lovina murmured, staring at the page as though the images of the boys themselves would appear in her mind's eye.

"I thought it best," came a soft voice from behind her.

Lovina jumped, knocking her water glass onto the floor as she whipped around.

Miriam stood at the open back door, her expression shuttered, her posture bolt upright. She made no move to come inside.

Before she could say anything, Lovina heard footsteps in the hall.

"What was that?" John started to say as he entered – and then stopped, when he saw Miriam.

He paused, mirroring Miriam's position in the opposite doorway. He looked from her to Lovina, and to the broken glass on the floor.

"Lovina?" he said uncertainly. "What – "

And then Miriam said the last thing Lovina would have expected her to: "She knows."

"What?" said John again.

"*What?*" echoed Lovina, shocked in her turn. She looked at John. "You know? About the children?"

"Miriam told me," said John, taking a compulsive step into the room and glancing at the as-yet unmoving figure of the widow herself. "How do *you* know?"

Lovina gestured at the directory on the table. Then she turned back to Miriam.

"No, wait," she said. "How did you know – that I knew?" She was too flustered to think of a better way to phrase the question.

"I was at the gift shop," said Miriam quietly. "In the stockroom. I heard you talking."

"What were you doing there?" asked Lovina, still feeling accusatory.

"I sell quilts," said Miriam.

Lovina could not think of anything to say to that, so she looked at her father. His gaze was still squarely on her. He did not look angry, not exactly. Lovina almost wished that he did, she felt as though she could do with an argument. Miriam was being entirely too calm.

"Lovina," said John gently. "Why didn't you just talk to me about this?"

Lovina narrowed her eyes slightly. "When did you give me a reason to?" she demanded. "How can I talk to you when you never talk to me?"

John flinched.

"I know you two are courting," Lovina went on. "I had to find out from *Sadie.* Who was so surprised that I didn't know, what with us being so close, and all each other has."

John bowed his head for a moment. "I'm sorry, Lovina. I was trying to... protect you, I guess."

Lovina bit her lip as he looked down.

"You were trying to protect each other."

Lovina looked over at Miriam, surprised to hear her chiming in. She nodded.

"I was trying to protect you, *daed*," she said. "I didn't want to tell you what I suspected until I was sure. But I guess I wasted my time. You're the only one that *wasn't* being lied to."

She turned back to Miriam. "I'm glad my *daed* knows the truth, at least," she said. "Were you ever going to tell anyone else?"

Somehow, strangely, this exchange with her father had calmed Lovina. She did not feel so angry as she had before. As her thoughts cleared, she could see the sadness in Miriam's expression. And even though she knew now beyond a doubt that her suspicions had been correct, Lovina could not help but feel her heart going out to the widow.

"Ask her why," John prompted softly. "Why she sells quilts."

Lovina looked curiously at Miriam.

"I'm saving," she said. "I want to bring my boys out to live with me."

"And... why aren't they with you now?" asked Lovina.

The older woman sighed softly, and finally took a step into the kitchen.

"They're with my brother. He's shared legal guardianship with me since my husband died. I was living there too, but my brother is... unkind."

Miriam's eyes flicked downward, and she moved a hand up to her throat. As Lovina realized what Miriam meant, she felt her stomach drop slightly. She glanced at her father, whose jaw was set.

"He had been bad-tempered when we were growing up, but it was worse when I started keeping house for him. I thought I could deal with it, I didn't have anywhere else to go. But then the boys, they started to defend me. David, the oldest, especially. He got hurt."

Miriam clasped her hands tightly together.

"But Jay loved the boys, he never raised his voice to them once on their own account, let alone his hand. It was only when they got between him and me."

There was a pause.

"So you left," said Lovina softly.

"I've been trying to get money together so I can bring them over," said Miriam. "And I had to change my name so Jay wouldn't be able to find us. He'd take them back if he did, I wouldn't be able to fight him."

"But I suggested," said John, walking over to stand next to Miriam, "that if Miriam were to marry, the boys would become part of her husband's family."

He placed a hand on Miriam's shoulder; the two of them looked at Lovina, worry etched across their faces. They were waiting for her approval.

And, as the last of her anger fluttered away, Lovina nodded slowly.

"That... seems like a good solution," she said.

She saw both her father and Miriam visibly relax. John smiled at Miriam; a warm, wide smile. Miriam blushed as though she were Lovina's age. They really did love each other, Lovina realized. Even without the problem of Miriam's children, they would have been married. Of course they would.

"So you'll be married in Fall," said Lovina. A troubling thought struck her. "But then you won't be able to fetch the boys until November at the earliest."

She thought, perhaps, that she should slow down and process everything, before looking to solve any more problems.

But then, what was there to process? Her father would remarry. And she would get to know Miriam – and the boys, when they got here – and they would become a family.

It was not a future that Lovina would have been able to recognize before this moment, but it was one she thought she could soon learn to love.

"That's months without seeing them," she said. "How long since you saw them last?"

"A week before I arrived here," said Miriam, her voice shaking almost imperceptibly. "I call David once a week from the tourist shop

– he sneaks out to the neighbor's barn, they've a phone in there – since I left, Jay's kept such a close eye on them, that's all the contact we can manage."

Lovina looked at her father – and considered, for a moment, how she would feel in that situation.

Then: "I have an idea," she said.

***

Lovina ran to the driver's side door and knocked on the glass.

"Tom," she panted, as he rolled down the window, "they've found a gap in the hedge behind the house, it's out of sight of the yard. Can you reverse back around that corner?"

Tom looked back at where she was pointing and rolled his eyes.

"I can turn around and drive forward around the corner," he said. "Whoever heard of reversing around a corner? And even if I did, I wouldn't do it in a minivan. Honestly, you're lucky I agreed to drive this thing at all."

Lovina just nodded, knowing that he did not expect an answer. She paused for a moment, peering over the tall board fence to see if her father was managing to distract Jay. Yes, it looked like they were still talking. John had agreed to pretend that he was lost and needed directions, and Miriam had provided him with a list of topics to use to keep the conversation going.

Lovina started back the way she had come, to where Miriam was helping the boys to make their way quietly across the back yard and through the gap in the hedge.

She was interrupted by Tom calling after her.

"Tell them to bring snacks if they want," he said. "I'm not stopping once we're off, just in case whats-his-name calls the cops. I've got some chocolate if they're desperate."

"Sure," said Lovina.

And despite Tom's worries, she could not bring herself to be concerned. She knew in her heart that they would make it. She had said as much to Miriam during the long drive here in the early hours of the morning. They had held hands in the gray dawn, and Lovina had promised that this would work. Of course it would. It had been her idea, after all.

She smiled as she ran back toward her new family.

THE SHY AMISH MAN

SAMANTHA COLLIER

Rebecca's eyelids were drooping. Then the yawn came, long and low.

Mrs Helmuth, sitting to her left, started choking on her coffee. "Rebecca Beiler!"

But she couldn't help it. She had been up since five this morning, in preparation for her little sister's wedding day. It was four o'clock in the afternoon now, and the force of her eyelids was almost too much.

"Your *kapps* is eschew, Rebecca," Mrs Helmuth continued. The woman's eyes raked over her, assessing every imperfect detail. Why, oh why, had she drawn the short straw and been seated next to the district matchmaker and gossip?

Yes, her prayer cap had slipped. Stray dark curls were escaping from it. Her black dress, ironed hastily this morning, was now as wrinkled as Mrs Helmuth's face. But she wasn't the only one showing signs of wear.

Annie, the bride herself, was smiling fixedly. Levi, her new husband, was sweating as if it was a scorching summer's day, rather than a chilly one in late November. Rebecca could see their hands intertwined beneath the table, though.

Celery stalks, the traditional Amish wedding decoration, were wilting in their vases. The last of the season's brown autumn leaves fluttered onto the tables, and a bitter wind was whipping napkins into the air. The salads were drooping in their bowls. The hog in the middle of the wedding table was shrivelled. Children whined, clinging to their parents.

Hours to go, before she could make her excuses, leave the tables under the trees and climb the stairs to her room. There was still singing and storytelling after the banquet ended.

At least the wedding was at their own farm. Rebecca offered up a silent prayer: Thank you, Lord, for small mercies.

Mrs Helmuth heaved. She sounded like an out of tune piano accordion when she spoke. The whole table shook as she leaned across it, grabbing Rebecca's hand in her short pudgy one.

"A very busy day, my *lieb*. It is hard, is it not, seeing your little sister married, while you still occupy a single room in your parent's house?"

Rebecca flinched as if she had been slapped. Stop it, she said to herself. She doesn't mean it in a nasty way. She is just concerned that I will never marry. It is normal. It is the way of things. Oh, Lord, please give me the strength to endure it.

"Oh my dear, I didn't mean to distress you," Mrs Helmuth said, patting Rebecca's hand. "It just makes me so sad to see such a lovely and humble girl like you with no husband of her own. And I am here to change that for you!"

"What do you mean?" Rebecca couldn't quite keep the thread of alarm out of her voice.

"I mean, my dear, that I have made it my mission to find you a husband!"

"Oh, Mrs Helmuth, I appreciate it, but..."

"No buts, my dear. I have it all sorted. I have arranged a date with a young man for this Saturday night!"

Rebecca felt her face redden. Why was Mrs Helmuth doing this to her? Didn't she realise that she would rather walk over hot coals than go on a blind date? This had to stop!

"Mrs Helmuth, thank you, but I couldn't possibly..."

Mrs Helmuth raised an imperious hand. "I won't hear another word. My promise to you is this: by this time next year, you will have a good husband, just like your sisters!"

There was nothing Rebecca could do. And she didn't notice the pointed look that passed between Mrs Helmuth and her mother, who were locking eyes across the souring sauerkraut.

"Excuse me." The hot sting of tears was pricking behind her eyes.

As soon as her bedroom door closed, she threw herself across her bed and the tears came like molten lava.

What a terrible promise to make to a girl in her position! If only Mrs Helmuth knew the secrets buried in her heart. She could date all the men in the world, but she still wouldn't find the husband that she wanted. There was only one man for her.

And he wasn't here. She had looked all afternoon, strained her neck every time someone new had come, shuddered at the sound of boots on the hallway steps. Every yellow haired man had made her look again. All to no avail. She should have known. He rarely came to social events.

She had known him forever, as you knew everyone in her close Amish community. She had gone to school with him; she had attended church services with him; she had participated in Evening Sings with him, back when she was a teenager.

She had not seen him much during *rumspringa*, when the young people 'ran around', before making the decision to be baptized into the church and hopefully remain forever in the community. She had heard that he had gone away, and there were rumours he might not return. But he had. He was as much a part of their community as she was now.

Samuel.

Even saying his name, in the privacy of her own bedroom, under her breath, caused her to shiver. Then there was her joy at seeing the old worn green and white sign to his shop: Fisher's Bakery. The jingle of the bell as the door opened, and let her inside. The sound of his laughter from the back of the store, as he baked. Flour on the shop bench. Heat spreading from the ovens to the shopfront. She would crane her neck to see out the back, and always failed. But she knew he was there.

Afterwards, the explosion of sugar on her tongue while biting into one of his sugar cookies. Her favorite.

She sniffled into her pillow. She let her mind drift back to that one special day many years ago, when he had spoken to her...

It always dawned rosy on Apple Butter Day. The milk from the cows tasted sweeter. The cheese had extra bite. Even the eggs were yellower than normal.

Apple Butter Day had been a tradition in their community forever. It was like a holiday, and something that Rebecca looked forward to every year. It was held at a different community member's house each year, and that year it had been her families turn.

The neighbours gathered, and everyone started peeling the mountain of apples for the butter. Children ran in and out of the kitchen, laughing, their mothers shooing them away. The huge copper kettle had been brought out and set up over the wood fire. They had all taken turns stirring that huge kettle, to make sure that the butter didn't stick.

Samuel had come in for a glass of water. She hadn't noticed him behind her at the water pump. When she did, she flushed and glanced down, in shyness but also in demut (humility). She had expected him to take a glass and start pumping water. But he hadn't.

She looked up at him.

He was staring at her. The pale blue of his eyes looked like sky on a clear summers morning.

Then he spoke.

"For lo, the winter is past, the rain has come and gone," he said.

Then he poured his water and left.

Why was that memory haunting her now?

She had not known what he meant when he had said it to her. Was it a farming reference? Her studies had led her to the Song of Solomon, where she had found the quote nestled in amongst other words of beauty and wisdom. But still – what was he referring to?

Why couldn't she let it go? Why did it stay with her?

Sometimes she dreamed that she would walk into his bakery, and ask him outright. "One sugar cookie, please, and what did you mean about the rain coming and going?"

But she never did. The memory was fading slightly, like an old photograph yellowing with age.

He never even acknowledged her, any more.

She could hear footsteps on the stairs leading to her room. It would be her mother, or one of her sisters, come to fetch her back to the wedding. Telling her she had to stop being so sensitive. That she had to stop running away. What they had been telling her forever.

Taking a deep breath, she stood up and left the room, hastily wiping away the tears with the back of her hand.

***

"Rebecca! Keep still!"

The stool wobbled beneath her bare feet. Her mother had already stuck two pins into her as she hemmed her best dress. Saturday night was here, and her date was about to arrive.

"I don't want to go."

"You are going, my girl." Pins in mouth, her mother's voice sounded muffled. "Even if I have to drag you there myself."

"I don't want to date. I don't even know who this David Graber is! He isn't from our district."

Mrs Beiler pulled at the dress. "He moved here a year ago. To help his poor uncle with the carpentry after the heart attack." She pulled at the dress again. "Oh dear. I hope this dress length passes the *Ordnung* rule. I might have hemmed it a bit high."

Rebecca's dark eyes flashed. "It isn't seemly for me to be seen with a man at Shauffer's Restaurant. Especially in a dress that is too short. People will talk!"

"My, my, what a prissy little miss you are." Her mother was squinting at the needle in her hand, attempting to re-thread the last bit of cotton. "Lots of young couples go to Shauffer's now. It is perfectly respectable. You sound like an old Amish *grossmammi*! Do you want to just buggy date?"

"Nothing wrong with buggy dating," Rebecca huffed. "A thermos of hot cocoa, some sugar cookies...sounds perfectly lovely!"

"Are you twenty-two or sixty-two?"

Rebecca snorted. It seemed to come out of her nose like steam.

She tried a different tack. "The weather is turning. There will be a snowstorm tonight!"

"Rebecca, there is nothing wrong with dating," her mother said. "Both your sisters are married now! I worry about you, my girl. You need to socialize more."

"I go to the Evening Sings!"

"You do not. You haven't been in over a year. You sit at home with me making quilts, that is all!"

"But..."

"*Nein*." Mrs Beiler was firm. "Hop down from that stool, your dress is ready. Go and put your *kapps* on, get your bonnet and cape and go and wait for him in the front parlour. You are going on this date even if I have to drag you there myself!"

***

Stop it, Rebecca said to herself. *Stop comparing them.*

But she couldn't help it. David's fingers were short and stubby, with a large amount of hair on them. Samuel's were long and beautiful – hadn't she watched them knead bread a million times when she had gone into his bakery? David's ginger hair was thin and receding slightly, while Samuel's was plentiful, and the colour of the corn in the fields on a bright summer's day. She didn't much care for David's table manners, either. He was scoffing his chicken pot pie like one of her father's pigs at the trough.

You concentrate on insignificant things, she scolded herself. *A man's character is more important than such vanity. Oh, Lord, please forgive this silly woman her pettiness.*

His pie smelt delectable, much better than the borscht she had ordered. But then, no one made borscht like her mother.

"How is your food?"

She looked up at him from her bowl, almost dropping the spoon in alarm. He wanted to talk!

"Fine, thank you."

An awkward silence. His ginger hair seemed to rise slightly from his head, as if it had been attacked by static electricity. She stared at him in distaste.

A figure loomed over their table. The waitress, of course, coming to ask them if they wanted dessert. Not if she could help it.

Except it wasn't the waitress. It was Samuel.

She flushed, turning the colour, she imagined, of one of the beets in her mother's vegetable garden. And her mouth was dryer than the sandpaper in her father's work shed.

"David," Samuel said, standing over the table. "I've been meaning to talk to you about your order of the pies for Christmas."

Samuel hadn't so much as glanced in Rebecca's direction.

"*Jah*, Samuel, could I pick it up on the twenty-second?" David responded.

"We are a bit understaffed now," Samuel said, then turned slightly and saw Rebecca.

He stopped, staring. The moment stretched on.

David watched them. "*Jah*, and is the twenty-second not good then?" No response. "Samuel? Do you know Rebecca?"

Samuel nodded, as if trying to dislodge a troublesome thought.

"*Jah*, Rebecca and I went to school together. I haven't spoken to her since we attended the Apple Butter Day two years ago."

Why was he talking about her as if she wasn't there? Rebecca wondered. It was probably just as well - she couldn't have trusted herself to speak. She was trembling like an autumn leaf about to fall from the tree.

David continued to look bewildered. "*Jah*, well, apple butter making is always good," he replied slowly. "About the order -?"

Samuel started.

"*Jah*, as I was saying, we are understaffed now and are snowed under. Literally!" he laughed, gesturing to the pale flakes swirling to the ground outside. "Could we possibly push it back to Christmas Eve?"

David nodded. "If it helps you, it shouldn't be a problem."

Samuel smiled. It was the first smile she had seen on his face since he had walked through the door. Samuel smiling was like a beam of sunshine breaking through a cloud on an overcast day. It made her want to bask in the warmth of it.

"Thank you, David," he said. "So much appreciated!" He paused, glancing at Rebecca.

"I shouldn't be disturbing your meal. I should go now."

Turning suddenly, he knocked the pepper shaker on the edge of the table. He grabbed for it at the same moment as Rebecca, who reached out her hand to save it tumbling to the floor.

Their hands touched.

Samuel gasped, his eyes narrowing.

He put his black felt hat back on his head and strode out of the restaurant.

David's mouth dropped open.

"What was that all about? That Samuel Fisher is an odd fellow, that's for sure. I remember talk that he lost his way during *rumspringa* and many expected that he wouldn't get baptized. I wonder if that contact with the outside world accounts for his strangeness?"

Rebecca was silent.

"Yes, well, we should probably get you home before the worst of this snow sets in. Ready to leave?"

More than ready. Her hand felt like it had been electrocuted.

She could barely stop it from shaking.

I have never felt anything like this in my life, she thought. *Pity Samuel hates me.*

***

The notes from the hymn rose to the top of the barn and hovered there like minnows in flight.

It was one of Rebecca's favourite hymns, and in that moment, nothing else existed.

She sang with all her heart. A song of joy and praise for our Lord. Time seemed suspended. In these moments, she felt as close to God as she ever could be.

Why had she stopped attending the Evening Sings? How could she have forgotten this special communion with God?

The final notes of the hymn stretched out, then ended. The boys and girls leaned across the table to each other. The sound of chatter filled the air.

It was always like this at the Evening Sings. The girls, in their church going frocks, at one side of the table. The boys, in their Sunday best, on the other. It was a different atmosphere to the service that had taken place here earlier. For a start, the hymns chosen were always livelier than the ones at the service. Rebecca loved the old, solemn hymns sang at the service – *Lob Lied* and *Amazing Grace* always brought a tear to her eye. But the Evening Sing hymns affected her differently. They made her want to shout out her love for the Lord to the world!

In between the hymns, the boys and girls would chat. And at the end, everyone would socialize for another hour or two. Often, a boy would take a girl home in his buggy. It was how the Amish courted. Rebecca had been to many as a teenager, as all Amish teenagers did. But she never chatted with any of the boys, and so never had anyone suggesting a ride home in his buggy to her. She hadn't minded. Her heart was always full of Samuel.

But he had rarely attended the Evening Sings, and hadn't spoken to her when he had.

It had been a long time since she had been to one herself. They were for teenagers. And she was an aging spinster, letting life and love slip her by.

The lovely euphoria the hymn had left her with punctured like a tack in a bicycle tire. She shouldn't have come. It was only at the insistence of Mrs Helmuth that she had.

The matchmaker had visited after the date with David, of course. "Well, my *lieb*, how did it go?" she had asked, as she settled at their kitchen table with a slice of her mother's apple pie and a coffee. Rebecca and her mother were putting the final touches to some quilts they were making.

"Terrible," Rebecca replied.

Why sugar coat it? The encounter with Samuel had ousted David completely from her mind. She had returned home that night convinced Samuel hated her. Why else would he have reacted the way he did when their hands touched, as if the slightest contact with her revolted him? And then to leave without saying goodbye.

Mrs Helmuth had coughed. "*Jah*, well, I have spoken to David," she said. "He seems to think that you are not a good match. He said he could barely get a word out of you. Rebecca, you have to try harder if you are ever going to get a fine husband and have a beautiful *bobbeli* of your own!"

"Well, maybe I am happy being here with my mother," Rebecca replied, a touch defiantly, then instantly regretted it.

Her mother raised an eyebrow at her over the quilt she was hemming. "Rebecca, remember respect."

"I am sorry, Mrs Helmuth." She felt her face burning as she looked down at her own quilt.

Mrs Helmuth's arms jiggled as she set down her coffee cup. "I do this for your own good. Remember my promise to you? Anyway, there are finer fish in the sea than have ever been caught. We will put David Graber behind us. This time you are going out with Timothy King. You know Timothy – the tall man who works at the dairy?"

She knew Timothy, and had never much liked him. And after another painful date, she had no desire to see Timothy ever again.

Next, Mrs Helmuth had pressured her into attending the Evening Sing.

"You haven't been for a while. It is time."

And so here she was. Mainly because her mother and father had left her behind after the service.

The next hymn started up, but Rebecca's heart wasn't in it anymore.

Her mouth moving but her mind distracted, Rebecca felt a fission of awareness. Someone was watching her.

Turning her head slightly to the far end of the table, she jumped. Samuel was sitting there, singing, but staring straight at her. When had he slipped into the barn? He surely hadn't been there when they had begun.

Their eyes met and locked. For Rebecca, it felt like everyone else in the room had melted away, and it was just the two of them, singing to our Lord and staring at each other.

Then it dissolved. He looked away, and the voices of all the others came back into her consciousness.

With a mumbled apology, Rebecca stood up quickly and left the barn. It was a dark, moonless night and she couldn't see her hand in front of her. Snowflakes drifted and fell upon her, cooling her skin. She raised a hand to feel her forehead. What was wrong with her? Was she getting a fever?

"Rebecca."

She turned to see a figure silhouetted against the gaslight of the open barn door. Was it him?

"My name is Eli Lapp, Rebecca. Is everything alright? You left the barn so quickly."

It wasn't him.

Rebecca forced a smile. "*Jah*, I just needed some fresh air," she replied. Disappointment pierced her heart.

Eli smiled. He was a tall, thin man with slightly bulging eyes. He held out his hand to her.

"I was going to introduce myself to you at the end of the night," he said. "Mrs Helmuth spoke to my mother about you, and suggested I talk to you. But if you are feeling a bit unwell, perhaps I might suggest I take you home now?"

Rebecca's heart sank. Mrs Helmuth. Of course. But she couldn't go back into that barn, and he was offering a way out.

"*Jah*, you are very kind," she replied.

She let him take her hand and lead her to his buggy.

As he helped her getting up, Rebecca didn't see that another figure had come to the barn door and was watching them. Nor, in the dark of the night as they trotted away, did she see that figure stay there watching. And kept watching, until the buggy was a tiny dot on the snow covered plain.

***

There was something magical about the lead up to Christmas, Rebecca always thought.

With only a few weeks to go, she was helping her mother with the Christmas baking. It was something that she and her sisters had done since she was small, and Rebecca looked forward to it every year.

Today the smell of almond cookies baking was permeating the air, and she was preparing a batch of walnut kisses to put into the wood oven. Her mother was stirring the mixture for sand tarts in a big ceramic bowl. Tomorrow they would bake pfeffermusse and Belsinckle Christmas cookies.

The snow had intensified, blanketing the farm in a thick layer of white. Rebecca almost sank into it when she had to go outside to do her daily chores, including milking Amelia, their docile cow. The weather was forcing passive activities on them. Mostly they quilted.

"Pass the milk jug, please Rebecca," Mrs Beiler asked, pausing in her stirring. Rebecca complied.

"So." Her mother wiped her hands on her apron. "Is Eli taking you out tomorrow night?"

Rebecca stopped what she was doing. "*Jah*."

Mrs Beiler shot her a piercing look. "You don't seem happy about that. Is Eli a good man?"

Rebecca shrugged. "Good enough, I suppose. He has bad breath, though, and – and – he pulls his fingers so the joints pop." She shuddered.

Her mother rolled her eyes and put down her spoon.

"Rebecca, there is something I want to say to you." She paused, as if choosing her next words with care. "You know that I love having you here with me. Since your brothers and sisters have married, it is wonderful to still have one of my children at home. It will be lonely when it is just your father and I rattling around this big house."

"You know I love being with you, Mamm."

"Yes, I know that my *lieb*." She reached out and patted Rebecca's hand. "But I must not be selfish. God does not smile on selfish women. I worry about you. You have always been my little lamb, hanging back. The others tore through life, full of confidence and bravado! Maybe I have over indulged you. You were always so timid, hiding behind my apron. But it has to stop."

Rebecca stopped cutting out the dough, and turned to her mother. "What do you mean, Mamm?"

Mrs Beiler took a deep breath. "I mean, you have to get out and find yourself a husband, Rebecca. You must try to be more social. That is why I spoke to Mrs Helmuth..."

Rebecca stared. "You were the one that set Mrs Helmuth up to harass me with dates!"

"Well, yes, but only for your own good..."

Rebecca didn't hear her mother. She had already walked away, climbing the stairs to the familiar comfort of her room. She tried to stop the tears from falling.

It wasn't that she didn't understand why her mother had approached Mrs Helmuth on her behalf. It was her duty to guide her daughter through life, and part of that was fielding courtships.

It was more that she felt disappointed in herself. She was failing as a dutiful daughter. She was a burden on her aging parents. She was a cripple. An emotional cripple.

She was disappointed that she could think only of Samuel. It was how it had always been, and why she had never gone on dates or pursued other boys.

But all that had to change. She was building her life on a foundation of tissue paper. Samuel had never expressed any interest in her. Granted, she had never given him much opportunity. Her love for him was based on one enigmatic comment from years ago.

The pepper shaker incident on her disastrous date with David showed that Samuel not interested in the slightest. In fact, he actively disliked her. He was revolted at her touch.

In need, she picked up her treasured Bible on her bedside table. Her rock, her comfort, her guide through life. Help me, Lord, she thought as she opened it. The beautiful words of 1 Corinthians 13: 11 confronted her:

When I was a child, I spoke as a child, I understood as a child, I thought as a child: but when I became a man, I put away childish things...

I put away childish things.

Closing the good book softly, she knew what she must do.

***

"Eli! Slow down! I am getting scared."

Rebecca was travelling with Eli in his buggy on an isolated country road. They were on the way to Rebecca's home after a date at Stauffer's in town. The night was as black as ink. Snow was falling in increasing intensity, and the ice on the road was making the wheels of the buggy slip and slide. Rebecca gripped the seat, trying not to lurch from side to side as the buggy swayed.

Eli was intent on what he was doing. "What did you say? I can't hear you in this wind."

Suddenly she was in the air, tumbling toward the embankment. Then all was still.

She awoke to the sound of horses whinnying pitifully. What happened? Where was she?

Stumbling, she attempted to claw her way back up the embankment. She could see nothing.

Then it all came rushing back into her mind.

We must have had an accident. Where is Eli?

She found her footing and managed to get to higher ground. The buggy was lying on its side; one wheel at a distance from it, still spinning. It must have come off, causing the accident. She couldn't see Eli anywhere.

"Rebecca! Are you hurt?"

Where did the voice come from? She didn't understand anything that was happening. Then she saw. A second buggy was further away, and a man was approaching her. Her brain didn't seem to want to work. I am having the strangest dream. I am on the side of the road, in the dark. I have had an accident. Samuel is here.

Samuel is here?

Yes, it was true. The figure approaching her was Samuel. Her heart filled with gladness to see him.

He was in front of her now, his face creased in concern. Then it changed to horror.

"You have blood all over you!"

Puzzled, Rebecca did nothing but stare at him. What was he talking about? She looked down at herself. Blood stained her best dress. She hadn't even known.

"Sit down, quickly, and I will have a look." Samuel held out his hand to assist her.

They found a spot by the side of the road. Rebecca sat down gingerly. "May I?" he asked, as he bent to lift her skirt. Rebecca shook her head. "*Nein*!"

"Rebecca, I have to see what's happened. We must stop the bleeding. There is no time for this."

With a pained sigh, she complied. The bleeding was coming from a large gash on her left leg. Samuel looked around. "Your cape. Pass it to me." He spoke softly but firmly. "And take off your shoe and stockings."

She took it off. He grabbed it, then ripped it in half, then again. Eventually he had a bandage he could use.

She was shivering now. The air was cold on her exposed leg. Samuel gently raised it, tying the ripped piece of cape around the wound. Snowflakes fell on her exposed skin, but his hands were warm.

"Stay there. Keep that leg raised." He looked around, finding a rock which he gently eased under her foot to keep the leg up. "Now, who were you with? You weren't driving the buggy alone at this time of night, were you?"

Rebecca shook her head. "*Nein*. I was travelling with Eli Lapp. I don't know where he is." She looked around, seeing nothing in the black of the night. He squatted beside her, putting an arm around her shoulders.

"It's alright. I will find him. Stay here."

He got up and walked away, calling Eli's name.

She drifted off. Next thing she knew, he was beside her.

"Now, Rebecca, listen. I have found Eli. He is on the other side of the road. He is drifting in and out of consciousness, and has a large bump on his head. I am going to put him in the back of my buggy, then I will come back and help you to it. Do you understand?"

Rebecca nodded. Her leg was beginning to throb.

After what seemed like an eternity, he returned and gently helped her to her feet. "Eli is in the back. Put your arm around me. Try to keep off that leg as much as possible."

She hobbled to his buggy, his arm around her. It felt natural, and good. It was ridiculous that she was thinking of that after all that had happened. Poor Eli was lying in the back of the buggy, moaning.

Samuel settled her next to him, putting his coat around her shoulders. And then they were on their way, driving past the wreckage of Eli's buggy.

"So what happened?" Samuel's voice interrupted her reverie.

When Rebecca finally found her voice, it sounded small and croaky. "The wheel came off."

Samuel looked at her sideways. "I know that. I mean, what caused it?"

Rebecca glanced at the still figure in the back. Eli appeared to be asleep. "I really don't know. The road is very icy."

"Yes, it is," Samuel agreed. "Which is why I am driving so slowly." He looked at her again. "How fast was Eli going?"

Rebecca reddened. "I don't remember."

Samuel didn't respond. They travelled for a while in an uncomfortable silence.

"So how long have you been seeing him?"

She jumped. She had been starting to drift off again. "I don't know. We have had maybe three dates." What did he care?

"Right." Did she hear a note of frustration? "Are you serious?"

Rebecca turned. "Not that is any of your business, Samuel Fisher, but yes. We agreed that we would announce our engagement after Christmas." A slight exaggeration, but he wasn't to know any different. *I have put away childish things*, she thought sadly as she spoke. *That includes you, Samuel.*

The buggy slowed down. Rebecca was puzzled. "Why are we stopping?"

He stared straight ahead. The horses nickered, stomping their feet a little.

"Do you think that is wise? You hardly know the fellow." He wouldn't look at her.

She turned to him. "I will say it again. It really is none of your business."

His face twisted then, with an emotion she couldn't name. "I am only looking out for you, Rebecca. You shouldn't be hasty, when it comes to such an important decision."

"Yes, well, the decision is mine to make." She was appalled to hear that her voice was shaking. "I am twenty-two years of age, a burden to my parents. It is right and good that I should find a man to marry and start a family of my own."

"Twenty-two?" He was frowning. "Well, you are more ancient than Methuselah! You will be needing a walking stick soon, I dare say." She looked at him sharply. Was he teasing her? But his face was impassive.

She drew herself up a little. "Please drive on."

He smiled. "Yes, of course, madam." And on they went.

She awoke with a start. The buggy was stopping again, this time at the front of a farmhouse that she recognized. And then she realised that she was slumped up against Samuel. She must have fallen against him when she fell asleep.

She sat upright hastily, pulling at her dress as she did so. "Where are we?"

He was jumping down from the buggy. "At old Dr Shetters. It's the nearest place I could think of to get you to for help."

A light had come on in the house, and a figure was coming down the drive holding a lantern as he spoke. It was Dr Shetter himself, who had been the district doctor for the community for over fifty years and had only recently retired. Dr Shetter had delivered Rebecca and all her brothers and sisters. He was a much-loved pillar of the community.

"Greetings! What have we here?" asked the doctor as he approached.

Samuel walked up to him. "Greetings, Dr Shetter, and apologies for disturbing you at night," he said. "I have brought you Rebecca Beiler and Eli Lapp, who have had a buggy accident. Eli is in and out of consciousness, and Rebecca has a deep gash on her left leg."

The doctor was assessing both as Samuel spoke. "Right then, Samuel, if you could help carrying Eli into the surgery. Rebecca, wait here, we will be back for you."

Half an hour later, Rebecca was sitting in a cosy armchair near the hearth in the living room. She was nursing a hot cocoa that Mrs Shetter had made for her. Her leg had been stitched and bandaged expertly by the doctor, and was now raised on an ottoman. The doctor and Samuel were still in the surgery with Eli, who appeared to have gained consciousness.

The doctor and Samuel walked into the living room.

"Rebecca, Samuel has just been to the telephone shanty and called your parents," the doctor said to her. The *Ordnung* rule was that members must not have telephones in their houses. Instead, there was a wooden shanty with a telephone which they shared, located at a central point between properties. "They will be here to pick you up in half an hour."

"You're not taking me home?" The words flew out of her mouth before she could stop them. She could have kicked herself.

Samuel looked at her. "I'm afraid I must get going, in the opposite direction to your place."

She bit her lip. "Of course. Thank you so much for your help tonight, I don't know what we would have done without you."

His face was impassive. "It was my duty by the grace of our Lord," was his reply. Then he picked up his hat. He looked around at all of them. "Goodnight, then." He turned to go, then glanced at Rebecca. "And congratulations for your forthcoming engagement."

Rebecca felt her face burn brightly. "Oh, Samuel, that is too hasty..."

But he was already off, and old Mrs Shetter, who was a lovely lady, but well known as a rival to Mrs Helmuth as the district gossip, had swooped upon her. Demanding what on earth Samuel was talking about.

***

".... And so it was, that, while they were there, the days were accomplished that she should be delivered. And she brought forth her firstborn son, and wrapped him in swaddling clothes, and laid him in a manger; because there was no room for them in the inn...."

Mr Belier's voice was strong as he read the Christmas Story from the Gospel of Luke to his family on Christmas morning.

Rebecca was spellbound, as she always was. It was her favorite story in the world. She loved this Christmas tradition of her father reading from the family Bible, while the family gathered around him.

Today, her little nieces and nephews were sitting on the rug. Her father sat in his favorite armchair. The rest of the family were either sitting or standing as they liked. Candles illuminated the windows. Cut out stars and angels were hung on string above the fireplace, where a huge fire was roaring.

"And there were in the same country shepherds abiding in the field, keeping watch over their flock by night. And, lo, the angel of the Lord came upon them, and the glory of the Lord shone round about them: and they were sore afraid...."

Rebecca smiled. She knew the story by heart.

" And the angel said unto them, Fear not: for, behold, I bring you good tidings of great joy, which shall be to all people. For unto you is born this day in the city of David a Saviour, which is Christ the Lord."

A lump had formed in her throat now, and she tried hard to keep back tears. Such a moving story.

She looked out the window of the living room to the first morning light glistening on the snow. She could see the Nativity scene that had been constructed the previous week. The children had made the display. Carved from wood, it stood out against a painted background. It looked spectacular against the white of the snow. She could see the figure of Mary, bending over the manger. How must Mary have felt, giving birth to our Lord in a stable, having to lay him in a manger? The humility of the Lord's birth place made tears spring anew in her eyes.

Everyone was getting up from their seats now the story was over. There were still morning chores to do. Horses had to be fed, the pig sty raked out, eggs collected from the hen house. She alone stayed sitting as everyone moved off, feeling useless and frustrated.

It had been two weeks since the accident, and Dr Shetter still wouldn't let her resume her daily activities, even though her stitches had been taken out and she no longer needed help to walk. It was good in some ways. She had been spared going to sing carols at the local aged care centre, which always made her nervous.

"Patience, Rebecca," her mother told her, when she expressed her displeasure at her immobility. "It won't be forever. Thank the Lord that you were not injured more seriously. Think of poor Eli, still bedridden."

How could she do anything but think of poor Eli? Since Samuel had told of their impending engagement to the Shetters, word had of course spread. She had had numerous visitors during her convalescence. They wanted to ask about the accident, of course, but seemed more eager to hear details of her supposed forthcoming engagement.

She blushed at their inquiries. "Please, don't speak of it. There is nothing to speak of! Eli and I were dating, that is all." How she hated speaking of such personal things to acquaintances! How she resented Samuel for putting her in such a position.

Samuel. She had not seen him since he had rescued them. He hadn't even bothered to inquire how she was doing. She didn't care anymore; she knew now that she was over her infatuation with him. Thank the Lord. It was better this way, much better...

She didn't think about Eli. She knew that as soon as she had the doctors' orders that she could leave the house, she should visit him. Maybe after Old Christmas....maybe.

Everyone was coming back into the house after chores, ready to open their presents. The children were whirling around in excitement.

There was no Christmas tree, and the presents were simple, in keeping with their customs. Each person had drawn a name out of a hat, and made or bought a present only for them. Rebecca had picked her older brother Aaron, and watched now in anticipation as he opened his present from her.

"Thank you, Rebecca," her brother said, as he unwrapped the hand knitted scarf. "Perfect for this freezing weather!"

Rebecca's present was from her older sister, Miriam. She gasped when she opened the box. Inside was a beautiful pale blue china tea set. She looked at her sister, unable to speak.

"For your hope chest," Miriam said. Then added impishly: "I hear that you might be opening that chest once and for all soon, Rebecca!"

"Miriam! Such indelicacy," scolded their mother. Rebecca couldn't think of a word to say.

"It's not, Mamm," Miriam continued. "Everyone is talking about how Rebecca and Eli are going to announce their engagement after he is well. Isn't that right, Rebecca?"

Rebecca still couldn't find her voice. Answer yes or no, she thought to herself. But all she could do was sit there like the fool she was, blushing as always.

Mrs Beiler changed the subject. "So what is this we hear that young Samuel Fisher is selling his bakery and leaving the district?" she asked the assembled group.

Rebecca flinched. What?

Another of her brothers, Joseph, spoke. "It's true, apparently. Everyone knows he has been having trouble keeping up with his orders. He is away now, looking for a buyer."

I do not care, Rebecca told herself. I do not care!

"He's been gone ever since he helped Rebecca and Eli after the accident," Joseph continued. "No one expects him back before Old Christmas."

Looking down at the pale blue china tea set on her lap, Rebecca tried very hard not to weep.

In the afternoon, the children took their sleds outside. They had a great time careering down the hill, laughing. They would catapult themselves off, throwing snow at each other.

Watching them through the window from her sofa, Rebecca couldn't help but remember when she and her siblings had been the ones on the sleds. Such simple times. Sometimes she wished she could return to that simple time. All you had to think about was what fun you would have after your chores were finished.

I put away childish things.

She thought she was doing the right thing, encouraging Eli. She had let him hope that there was an engagement awaiting them. She always knew that she didn't love him, but she thought that love might grow in time. She needed to marry and start her own family, become independent of her parents. She thought she had resolved herself to this.

Why then was she so sad?

And Samuel. By all accounts, he had gone away, was selling up. What had happened to his business? The thought of never being able to go into Fisher's Bakery again and order a sugar cookie made her heart ache.

She had to put him behind her. There had never been anything between them, anyway. The most that they had spoken had been on the night of the accident, and that was only because he had been forced to converse with her.

She meant nothing to him. He was completely indifferent to her. No, it was worse than that – he disliked her. Let's not forget the pepper shaker incident at Stauffer's, she told herself.

Lord, she prayed, give me the courage to get over this man. And let me find the way to love another.

***

Today was her first outside walk since the accident.

Christmas Day had come and gone, but in Amish tradition, the extended family had stayed on. There had been lots of outside activities with the children. The whole family had joined them in building snowmen and having snowball fights. They were constantly on their sleds. And, one day, they had all gone ice skating at a local lake.

"Can I come today?" was her almost daily refrain. But everyone said no, that she had to keep resting her silly leg! It was so frustrating. Even though she knew that they were doing it out of love for her, she felt excluded.

So, today was extra special.

Miriam and Annie had gone a little way with her, before being called back to the house for various chores. Today was the Epiphany; or Old Christmas, as they called it. January 6th. As important as Christmas Day itself to the Amish, there would be a big feast and they all had to pitch in to help. She had shooed them away, saying she would be perfectly fine and wouldn't go far.

It was only a small white lie.

She had skirted the creek, and was now looking over the iced water. It was a beautiful day. A pale light was making the snow glisten. But she should have listened to them. She was beginning to tire, and there was nowhere that she could sit and rest in the thick snow.

She looked over the hill and could see a figure approaching: a tall man in black. Relief flooded through her. It was Joseph or Aaron, come to help her.

She started waving, and the figure saw her and started heading in her direction.

Her arm stopped waving and fell to her side. Confusion etched her features. It wasn't Joseph or Aaron. It wasn't her father. Nor was it Levi, Annie's husband, or Dan, who was Miriam's. This man was not part of her family.

This man was Samuel.

Was he lost? Why was he on their property?

He approached her slowly. He was wearing his black felt hat, which dimmed his yellow hair. White snowflakes glistened, then dissolved on his black coat.

"Greetings," he said. Then he stopped, two steps in front of her.

Rebecca drew her cape tighter around her, and thanked the Lord that she was wearing her bonnet, which concealed her face. Her heart had begun to race.

"Greetings, Samuel," she replied.

He didn't seem to be in any hurry to speak further, simply gazing over the meadow toward the house. Rebecca felt herself trembling. Oh, Lord, why is this so hard?

"Did you have a good Christmas?" she asked, just to break the silence. Inside, she wanted to scream.

He stared into her face.

"Good enough," he replied. "What about you and your family?"

"Lovely, thank you," she replied. "Are you selling your bakery?" She could have kicked herself once the words left her mouth. It was too direct.

"You've heard talk." He looked down at the snow-covered ground. "People gossip. No, I was never intending to sell. But I was worried about the business. I have been away, looking for a new baker to hire, that is all."

"Why are you here, Samuel?" she blurted.

"To see how you are, of course," he replied. "After the accident."

Suddenly, she couldn't stand any of it, anymore.

"Well, I am mending, as you can see," she replied tartly. "Are you satisfied? Will you leave me be now?"

She turned, and started walking away from him. He followed, grabbing her arm to still her.

"Are you mad with me?"

She ripped her arm away, her dark eyes blazing.

"Mad? Why should I be mad?"

"You are most definitely mad," he said. But his eyes were twinkling.

"Are you laughing at me?" She felt close to tears now.

"I would never laugh at you, Rebecca," he answered. He looked solemn. "I respect you far too much."

"Respect me?" she scoffed. "You don't even talk to me! You go out of your way to avoid me. You acted as though you had been poisoned when our hands accidently touched in Stauffer's!"

He took his hat off his head, and scratched it, looking down at the ground.

She burst into tears.

Straight away, his arms were around her, soothing her. She felt her tears drying on his hair. He was crooning, whispering soothing endearments to her.

She stilled. She had never been this close to a man, apart from her father and her brothers.

As if compelled, she turned her face up to him. Then couldn't look away.

The kiss when it came was slow and sweet. She had no idea a man's lips could be so soft.

It ended, and she stepped away, confused. Her first kiss.

"Rebecca, I am a stupid man," he said. "I came here today to try to talk to you about my feelings. But I have failed, as always. I know that you think that I dislike you, but it couldn't be further from the truth."

He took her hand, looking deep into her eyes. "I love you. I always have."

It felt like a dream. Was this happening? Would someone pinch her, and she would soon wake up? She thought she was standing on a hillside in the snow, and Samuel had just kissed her and told her he loved her.

"You love me?"

"Yes. With all of my heart."

"You love me," she repeated, in wonder.

"I knew that I loved you since that Apple Butter Day at your house, just before *rumspringa*. But once I realised, it was like I always knew. But I didn't know if you returned my feelings. You were always so shy! And I am like that, myself." He looked down at his feet.

"Oh, I know that people call me odd and say I am haughty, but really, it is because I don't know what to say or do around people most of the time. So, I keep to myself. I didn't know how to approach you. Every time you came into my bakery, I would look at you and long to speak to you. I would promise myself that next time you came in I would, but I always lost courage." He paused.

"And then I saw you dating a few men. When it became obvious that you were going on dates with Eli Lapp, I gave up, I am sorry to say. But I have been away and thought long and hard about it; I have prayed and prayed. The Lord has told me to approach you."

He took her hand.

"Rebecca, if you are serious about Eli then I will walk away from here today and never bother you again. Even though he is not much of a man! He did not take care of you properly that night. He was riding the horses too hard on the icy road. He caused your accident."

He glowered. "The thought of what could have happened to you has been tearing me apart!"

She looked up at him. He wanted to protect her. He said that he loved her! So, she forced herself to speak all that was in her heart.

"Samuel," she said. "I didn't want to date other men – it was my mother and Mrs Helmuth who made me! I have only ever wanted you. That is why I always came into your bakery."

"Not for my delicious sugar cookies?"

She laughed. "Your sugar cookies are delicious, but no, not just for them! But you never noticed me. I thought I was a silly woman, hoping where there was no hope. I needed to get married, so I thought maybe I could learn to love Eli. I tried! But it wasn't any good. I went to see him a few days ago and told him that I can't date him anymore."

He reached down and stroked a dark curl that had escaped her bonnet. "So you don't love Eli?"

She shook her head. Tears had sprung in her eyes again. "I love you," she said.

Suddenly, Samuel let out a holler and picked her up, whirling her around. "She loves me! She loves me!"

Rebecca burst out laughing. How could so much happiness be contained?

"I left Stauffer's that night, knowing for sure that you were my love," he said. "Brushing your hand was like coming home. It was like my body recognised yours." He shuddered.

"That is why I went to the Evening Sing. It was to see you again, and maybe approach you. I overheard Mrs Helmuth in the bakery, saying that you were going. But then Eli came to you..." His voice tapered off. He looked lost.

She couldn't bare it. She reached up to him and softly trailed her hand over his face. He turned to it, and kissed it softly.

"If only we knew," she whispered. They had loved each other, forever, but their shyness had kept them apart.

"Well, it is all good now," she smiled. "And maybe we can thank Mrs Helmuth for that."

He raised an eyebrow. "How so?"

"Well, if she hadn't forced me to go on dates with other men, you might never have got the courage to approach me." She looked at him shyly.

He grinned. "You could be right. We should thank her! She has done her job well – if only she knew it."

Rebecca looked around, and saw Aaron and Miriam in the distance, approaching them. They must have been drawn by Samuel's shouts.

"Others are coming," she whispered.

He drew himself up. "Shall we go and join them? I would like to come to your house and speak with your father, if I may." He looked down at her again. "Will you marry me?"

This couldn't be real. And yet it was. "I will," she breathed.

"Thank you, Lord," Samuel said. He turned his eyes to the sky, overcome with emotion.

They joined hands, then turned to face the others.

She stopped. "Samuel, what did you mean when you quoted the Song of Solomon? On Apple Butter Day."

He knew instantly what she meant. "I saw your face as I turned around. You were so beautiful! My heart was overflowing with the Lord's love." He paused. "I wanted to tell you that it was a new season, a new day." He blushed. "Maybe for us, by the grace of God."

"And so it is," she said. "By the grace of God."

Suddenly, it struck her: Mrs Helmuth had said she would have a fine husband within the year. A smile slowly spread across her face.

The matchmaker's promise had come true.

AN AMISH WILDFLOWER
TERRI DOWNES

Wildflowers

Daisy tapped against the porch railing with slight impatience, looking out at where the already pale sunshine was beginning to drain away. It would be dark in a couple of hours, and Sadie would no doubt already be waiting for her.

She heard steps approaching the house and turned, thinking that perhaps Sadie had come looking for her, but it was Andrew Miller, a friend of her eldest brother.

He greeted her pleasantly as he reached the porch.

"Jacob's on his way back," Daisy told him. "I saw him, Simon and the others headed over the pasture a minute ago."

She had thought, for a moment, of waiting here on the porch until they returned... not to see her brothers, but because she knew who would be with them. She had not seen him in so long. But if she greeted the boys and then left immediately, it would be obvious that she had stayed just to see *him*.

She expected Andrew to move on, maybe to go and meet Jacob as he arrived, but he paused. He offered a smile, which Daisy returned, a little confusedly. She had never really spoken to Andrew before, except in passing. What did he want?

"Actually, I was hoping to catch you here. I wanted to ask you something." He paused for a moment. "It's just, my *daed* said I could use the good buggy this winter, and, well..."

He looked down for a moment and shuffled his feet. Daisy's mouth opened in surprise. Was he... asking her to go courting? It seemed like it, although no boy had ever asked her before, so she lacked comparison points.

Should she say yes? He was handsome, but she did not knew him very well, and she had never felt any kind of attraction to him. Even so, would it be rude to refuse, especially as she had never received any other invitations?

These, and a hundred other thoughts, arrived in Daisy's mind all at once, before Andrew had even raised his head again. They were so distracting that she almost failed to hear the next sentence he uttered:

"Do you think that Sadie would be interested in going for a drive with me?"

Daisy realized that she had yet to close her mouth, and did so immediately. She then gave herself a moment before she spoke.

"Don't you think you should ask Sadie that?"

"Well, I would... I mean, I will, but she's not always so... friendly." Andrew said awkwardly.

"If you think that, why ask her at all?" asked Daisy, although she knew the answer already. She sighed, feeling bad for Andrew. "Listen, Sadie is friendly. It's just that she's mostly friendly toward people who actually know her. And asking me about it isn't going to help you, is it?"

She tried to sound encouraging, because he did seem a little helpless, though her feelings of embarrassment over her misunderstanding were already growing. What if she had started to accept before she realized what he had really been asking?

Then again, Andrew was now the one looking embarrassed.

Daisy turned back to the front door as she heard her younger sister Ruth approaching.

"Thanks. Next time ask before you borrow it, all right?" she said, holding out her hand and ignoring Ruth's surprised glance at Andrew, who appeared to be blushing very deeply indeed.

"Mine has a hole," said Ruth, handing over Daisy's woolen shawl. "I've tried darning it but that's only made it worse."

"You should have asked me for help," said Daisy.

"You've been so busy with the flowers," said Ruth, a little too petulantly for her thirteen years.

"We'll be finished in a few days," Daisy promised, and kissed Ruth's cheek. "Then I'll have all the time in the world to help you."

She said a polite goodbye to Andrew, who mumbled something back, and then escaped through the yard and into the back pasture.

The sky was marbled with clouds, and the hard, metallic scent of the first frost was just starting to suggest itself. Daisy sniffed appreciatively, and felt her cheeks begin to flush against the chill. She had enjoyed the summer hugely, and always loved the fall, but winter had its own beauties to be enjoyed.

Although it would be a shame that she and Sadie would once again have to put their project to bed until spring.

She reached the furthest point of the pasture and let herself through the small gate into an adjoining meadow. And, as she had predicted, Sadie was already there. She waved as she saw Daisy approaching.

"I thought you'd abandoned me!" she said in joking accusation as Daisy reached her. "Here, come on."

She held out one of two rakes that she had with her, though Daisy could see that a large section of the ground had already been set into neat, parallel lines.

"You started without me!"

"I was cold," said Sadie, rolling her eyes and handing Daisy the second rake.

The two girls began their work, raking over the top soil in light, even strokes. This was their project, their little business, which kept them busy spring, summer and fall. The meadow belonged to Daisy's father, though he had never found a use for it before Daisy suggested that she might be able to do something with the immense quantities of wildflowers that bloomed there every year.

Her father, always encouraging his children to be as industrious as possible, had liked the idea. He gave her permission to try the project, provided that she take full responsibility for everything. She had only been fourteen at the time, but had made a great success of her work. Her little posies had sold out at every market she brought them to, and her twisted brown paper packages of carefully labeled seeds had been equally popular.

The next year, she had brought on Sadie as a partner in the project. This past summer had been their most successful yet. Now, they were preparing the ground for its long winter sleep.

Daisy glanced over at Sadie as they worked. Her best friend was a bright spot in the otherwise desolate landscape. Not just because of her plum colored dress, but her glowing skin, her rich caramel colored hair, her large and limpid green eyes. Daisy usually appreciated Sadie's loveliness just as she would that of the foxgloves and poppies they grew in the meadow. But on days like today, she felt just as drab and washed out in comparison as the gray and brown scrub which surrounded them.

"What?" asked Sadie, pausing in her work when she saw Daisy looking at her.

"...I thought I should mention," said Daisy, "that Andrew Miller is probably going to ask you for a drive."

She related the story to Sadie. She knew that it might be just as inappropriate for her to tell Sadie as it was for Andrew to ask her such as question in the first place. But she could not help herself, for she knew what Sadie's reaction would be, and it was all she could think of that would drive the sting from her embarrassment.

It worked; Sadie laughed. She always did. She had caught the attention of just about every boy in their community at one point or another since turning seventeen at the beginning of the summer. She had blossomed with such decisiveness that Daisy had joked she was doing it intentionally to compete with the flowers.

But Sadie had not met the attention with joy. She had never been much for socializing. In fact, Daisy thought that she might be the only really close friend Sadie had ever had.

Whenever a boy asked her for a drive, she would thank him politely and decline. Then she would laugh about it with Daisy afterward – Daisy, who had turned seventeen a week before Sadie, yet remained as unappealing as it seemed she had always been.

Daisy tried to drive these thoughts from her head as she worked, talking with Sadie about their plans for the next week, and how they might expand the project the following year. Soon, however, it became too dark to work.

"Sorry again," said Daisy, as they headed home through the dusk. "I'll make sure to get an earlier start on Monday."

"It's not your fault," said Sadie. "Tell Ruth to leave your things alone next time."

Daisy shrugged. "It's a little my fault," she said. "I did tell her I'd help her darn her shawl. Anyway, I'll have more time on Monday. We might even get it all finished."

Sadie sighed. "I almost don't want to," she said. "I get so bored without the work, don't you?"

"I'm sure we can keep ourselves busy," said Daisy. "Maybe you should take Andrew up on his offer."

She laughed when Sadie gave her an affectionate push, though her conscience pricked her over mocking Andrew.

"Will I see you at Singing tomorrow?" she asked.

Sadie nodded. "Will you have space for me?" she asked. She was the only one of her siblings old enough to go to Singing, and her father never wanted to make the trip just for her.

"We're taking two buggies," said Daisy, "so yes."

"Oh, of course, Simon and everyone will have come back from Goldacre now," said Sadie, referring to the group of boys who had gone over to a neighboring community for the summer and fall as a work party, including Daisy's brother.

Daisy nodded. It was almost on the tip of her tongue to say the name she had thought of almost before her own brother's when she had heard of the group returning. The name she had thought of every day for more than a year.

But she could never bring herself to speak of boys with Sadie. It always felt so embarrassing, knowing that they never returned her affections, and in fact were more likely to be interested in Sadie. She did not like the idea of anything coming between them in that way.

Though, perhaps, she might speak to him tomorrow... for the first time in months. Perhaps he had missed her. Perhaps he would speak to her, ask how her summer had gone. Perhaps afterward she would ask Sadie's opinion about him...

Isaac.

***

She had forgotten.

Daisy had forgotten, in her eagerness to see Isaac, just how long it had been since they had last spoken.

It had been hard to clear her thoughts around Isaac. Daisy almost could not remember when she had started feeling the way she did about him. They had never spent time together, just the two of them, but they had become fairly good friends through youth group. Daisy had simply become more and more excited to see him each week, and to seek him out in groups, and to ask his opinion on everything.

She noticed, one day, that his was the first face she looked for at any gathering, by which time it was too late to prevent herself from falling in love; not that she would have wanted to prevent it. He was everything she could imagine an ideal partner to be.

Tonight would be the first time Daisy would see Isaac since spring. And she had not thought of what this would mean, until Simon, her brother, pulled her aside after the gathering.

"What is it?" she asked.

"I was wondering about Sadie," he said quietly, his gaze already trailing back to where the girl in question was standing.

"What about her?"

"Is she..." he lowered his voice. "Do you know if she's courting anyone? You don't have to give any details, I was just wondering."

Daisy sighed. "Why can't any of you just ask her directly?"

"Any of who?" Simon frowned.

"Never mind," Daisy said quickly. "But really, if you're interested just speak to her. Since when are you nervous to ask a girl out for a drive?"

"Normally, I'm not," admitted Simon. "But, I mean, look at her. She was always pretty, but I haven't seen her since spring. What a difference!"

"I know," said Daisy, turning and looking across the room along with her brother.

She expected to see, as she always did, Sadie talking to a boy. Or, rather, a boy talking to Sadie, while she looked around for an excuse to move on. Sometimes she would even catch Daisy's eye, as though asking for a rescue, at which point Daisy would come and interrupt. Sadie had said, once, that she would do the same for Daisy any time she wanted. Neither she nor Daisy had mentioned the unlikeliness of this ever happening.

And there, indeed, was Sadie. With a boy. But this time, she was not looking around in boredom or irritation. This time, she was smiling. This time, she was looking up at the one speaking to her, attentive, touching the hair tucked behind her ears in sweet self consciousness. She said something and blushed, and perhaps had never looked so lovely before.

Simon sighed. "Ah, that's always the way. As soon as I'm interested, they meet someone else." He laid his hand over his heart as though wounded, expecting Daisy to laugh at him.

Daisy did not reply. She was staring at the boy Sadie was speaking to. Tall, with a straight back and confident tilt to his chin, eyes that always seemed interested, a dimpled smile. Isaac, looking at Sadie the way Daisy had always imagined he might someday look at her.

She turned and walked away.

***

Due to Sadie's disinterest in the subject, and Daisy's lack of opportunity, they did not generally spend the ride home from Singing discussing which boys had been there and who had spoken to them, except to laugh over it. That night, however, there was no discussion of the kind at all.

Sadie was, in fact, unusually quiet.

Daisy allowed herself to hope that this meant she was not excited over seeing and talking to Isaac. She did not bring him up, or mention how long it had been since they had seen any of the boys who had gone to Goldacre. Surely, if she had been interested, she would have said something?

Of course she would have. After all, what had happened? They had talked. Nothing else.

But the next week, after Preaching, as Daisy was helping some of her cousins with the cleaning up, she saw them again. Isaac and Sadie. Isaac had still not spoken more than a couple of words to Daisy since his return, but he had apparently had enough to speak about with Sadie that he needed to get her exclusive attention. And again, she seemed to be receptive.

The next time, and the next, were the same. Daisy began to dread communal gatherings. In her more thoughtful moments, she wondered if she was making too much of all of this. Would she even have noticed Isaac and Sadie's interactions if she had not been looking for them?

And she could not stop herself from looking for them. Sometimes, she would accidentally catch Sadie's eye while she was talking to Isaac, and would have to smile as though she had intended it.

Sadie still had not said anything about Isaac. She and Daisy had not been spending so much time together without their flowers, but she still came over to Daisy's home fairly often throughout the winter. She had had plenty of time to say something.

This was what Daisy told herself, for those first weeks of winter. Ignoring the truth, denying it. And when she felt that she could not deny it any more, that she was simply waiting for Sadie to put her out of her misery, she began avoiding her friend. Unlike Sadie, she had many close friends in the community, and she kept herself engaged as often as possible. Even when the two friends did see each other, it was usually at a large gathering, unsuited to confidences.

It was a week before Christmas when the inevitable happened. Sadie had surprised Daisy, arriving unannounced. Not that Daisy had any reason to be surprised; since they were small, the two of them had run in and out of one another's kitchens as though they were their own. Daisy shooed her sisters Ruth and Mary, whom she had been giving a sewing lesson, away to practice on their own.

Sadie was hesitant as they sat down. Daisy filled the pause, and hid her shaking hands, by pouring them each a cup of tea.

"Mary made these scones," she said into the silence, pushing the plate forward. "She's started inventing her own recipes. In case you're worries, I have tried them, and I promise they're good."

She forced a smile. Sadie took one of the scones, almost without looking.

"I'm not sure if you've noticed," she said slowly, her long lashes lowering to her cheeks as she spoke. "But I've been spending some time with Isaac recently."

Daisy steeled herself. This had been bound to happen. *He had never shown any interest in you anyway,* she told herself.

Don't throw the teapot at her, she told herself.

"It would be hard to miss," said Daisy, her words measured carefully. "He's the first boy you haven't chased away with a stick."

Sadie laughed, and blushed. Her laugh, and blush, were both lovely. Everything about her was, Daisy thought. Even her fingers, clasped as Daisy's were around a teacup, were long and elegant. Daisy's were short and square-tipped.

"We've started courting," said Sadie, raising her teacup to her lips.

Daisy nodded. "I thought you might," she said, because she wanted to say something that was true.

"You don't mind, do you?" asked Sadie.

Daisy blinked. The question seemed to have come from nowhere. Sadie was gazing at her entreatingly. Nervously. Did she know...?

"What do you mean?" she asked, feeling her voice choke a little. She took a big gulp of tea.

Sadie glanced down at the table. "Well, it won't make a big difference now, in winter, but in spring when we're running the flower trade again then I won't have quite so much time... if we're still together. You know."

Daisy swallowed. So Sadie was already thinking long term. "Of course," she said. "I understand. It was bound to happen sooner or later."

"I'm sure it will get even more difficult to schedule when you're courting as well," smiled Sadie.

But at this, Daisy could not smile. This had always been prohibited talk between them. No matter how many boys spoke to Sadie, or asked her to drive or walk, she would never speak to Daisy about how she would get attention in her turn.

Don't pity me, Daisy wanted to hiss. Instead, she refilled their teacups.

***

Daisy leaned back against the wall of the Millers' kitchen. Despite the frozen night, the room where they had had Singing that evening had become uncomfortably warm with so many people crammed inside. And, she could only just admit to herself, she had wanted to avoid Sadie.

After her first internal reactions, she had regretted her hard thoughts toward her friend. Sadie had not known how she felt about Isaac. If she had, Daisy might have had cause to be upset. But as it was, Sadie had simply found the first young man she was interested in. And Daisy was the only friend she would want to speak about all of this with. So Daisy had tied up her jealousy, prayed for patience, and started asking Sadie all about how things here going with her suitor.

Sadie had clearly been grateful to have someone to share everything with. Sadie had started spending time at Daisy's home once more, often arriving early afternoon with a pile of mending and staying until evening while Daisy helped her sisters and heard her little brothers' lessons. Despite the pain caused by every story Sadie shared about Isaac, Daisy had stopped trying to avoid her – but now, she simply had to.

Isaac had seen Daisy as she had arrived, and had come over to speak with her. Her heart had leaped to her throat at the sight of him, and his voice had made her thoughts feel warm and liquid. For a moment, it was as though nothing had changed. But then it became apparent that he was only speaking to Daisy to ask her is she had seen Sadie.

She had felt her face burning all through Singing, and had had to escape.

"Daisy?"

Daisy pushed herself away from the wall hurriedly and found herself facing Emma Miller, Andrew's youngest sister. She looked concerned.

"Are you all right? Sadie was looking for you, she thought you went home."

"I'm fine," smiled Daisy. "Just needed a little quiet."

"Oh, sorry," said Emma, stepping away.

She was one of the younger girls that Daisy had been helping with her sewing this winter; sometimes, it felt as though Daisy had accumulated even more sisters.

Daisy laughed and caught her arm.

"I've had my quiet now," she said, "besides, I could hardly chase you out of your own kitchen, could I?"

Emma smiled. Then she glanced behind her, as though in secret. Her twelve-year-old face seemed oddly sober as she addressed Daisy.

"I was thinking," she said. "About your flowers. Next year. Can I help you with them?"

Daisy tipped her head to the side. "Well, sure you can, we can always use a little more help. You know much about wildflowers?"

Emma nodded eagerly. "I'm learning. And I want to learn more. I thought Sadie wouldn't like me joining in, cause I know she's kinda snappy with her little sisters."

Daisy laughed. "She's not that snappy, you know."

Emma looked dubious. "Well. Anyway, I figured you'd need some extra help when she gets married."

"When Sadie gets married?" Daisy repeated.

"I know it's always a secret," said Emma, looking behind her again. "But my brother said it's going to happen. He seemed kind of put out."

"Did he," said Daisy. Her mind seemed to be going more slowly than usual.

Emma sighed. "Sure did." She came over and leaned against the wall next to Daisy. "All this love stuff seems very difficult," she said. "I'd rather plant flowers like you, Daisy."

Daisy nodded silently.

"Say, is that why you like flowers? Cause your name is one?" asked Emma.

"It's, uh…" Daisy clasped her hands for a moment. She felt a dull ache along the lines of her pulse. "It's actually because of Sadie I'm called that."

"What do you mean?"

"I was born the week before, and my mother called me Sadie. That's my real name." It had been a long time since Daisy had told anyone this story. "But Sadie's mother was ill when she gave birth, and she and Sadie's father hadn't heard about my name. So they called her Sadie as well."

"So you got called Daisy… oh, that's like Sadie mixed up!" said Emma delightedly. "Why wasn't Sadie called Daisy though, if she came second?"

Daisy shrugged. She did not want to tell Emma of how stubborn and obstinate Sadie's mother could be, and how her own mother had agreed to a nickname to keep the peace. She also could not bring herself to articulate the dark thoughts that plagued her sometimes. Thoughts of resentment and self pity, deciding that it had all started then, with their names, that Daisy would always come second to Sadie even if she was supposed to be first. That Sadie would always be better, more accepted, a more legitimate version of Daisy.

It was unfortunate that she should have let these thoughts take her over at that moment. Because then, she walked back through the sitting room and onto the porch, where she saw Sadie and Isaac, standing as close as discretion would permit, with soft expressions on their faces, murmuring something low and loving. And when Sadie saw Daisy, her face suddenly changed, and she took a quick step away from Isaac. She looked guilty.

They had not been doing anything wrong. Sadie had not reacted until she saw that it was Daisy interrupting them.

Which meant, Daisy realized as she turned on her heel and fled, that Sadie did know. She had always known.

As Daisy away as swiftly as she could without running, resentment swelled up and crested over her like a wave.

***

"I haven't seen you in a while."

Daisy nodded, and held out the basket of preserves. She had not been able to come up with a reason for her mother that she should not be the one to bring them over; in fact, her mother had been under the impression that Daisy would be excited to see her friend.

She had been almost embarrassed over the fact that she did not want to tell her mother everything that had happened. Perhaps this was a sign that her feelings were unhealthy. But she had not been able to bring herself to speak of them.

Now, however, Sadie was looking at her with that earnest, nervous expression once more. She had not offered Daisy anything to eat or drink, but instead stood awkwardly in the middle of her kitchen, clutching the basket of preserves.

"It's been weeks," she said. "Since that Singing at the Millers'."

"I've seen you at Preaching since then," said Daisy.

"We've barely spoken."

This was true. Daisy had been avoiding Sadie as much as she could. She knew that if Sadie pushed the matter, she would not be able to keep silent. She had hoped that Sadie would know this – but it seemed that she did not.

Sadie licked her lips, and asked the unwise question:

"Are you upset about something?"

The wave broke. It flooded through every part of Daisy.

"Are you joking?" she asked, and she could swear her voice had never sounded so cold and flat before.

Sadie blinked, and took a small step backward. "What? I... I mean, you looked a little upset, when I saw you, at the Millers', I thought..."

"You knew."

"What?" Sadie said again, less certain this time.

"You knew. You saw me, and you looked guilty. You acted like you didn't know how I felt about him, but you did."

"I... I didn't..."

"Don't lie to me. *Don't lie to me.*"

Sadie drew a long, deep breath, and finally met Daisy's gaze head on. "I gave you a chance to say something. I asked."

"You asked if I minded you taking time away from the flower business. Why bother bringing it up if you weren't going to be honest about the question?"

"I didn't want to make you uncomfortable."

"What, by telling the truth?" snapped Daisy.

Sadie flushed. "I was trying to be considerate."

"If you were being so considerate, you would never have started seeing him."

Something heated and horrible seemed to be growing in the space between the two girls. Their thoughts could no longer be contained; every unpleasant feeling each of them had seemed to want to spill out.

"So that's your real answer, is it?" said Sadie. "That it doesn't matter what I want, or what Isaac wants, you liked him first so he's yours, even if he doesn't like you?"

Daisy flinched. Sadie pretended not to see as she continued.

"Don't pretend that you were calmly letting all of this go. I've seen you looking at us. You've been acting as though I stole something –

something that wasn't even yours to begin with. You could have just said something."

"And you could have acknowledged that this would hurt me. You could have taken a step back, so that I didn't have to hear how every drive with him went, and every conversation." Daisy felt her face grow hot. "You don't have to remind me that I never had a right to expect anything from Isaac, *thank you,* but you didn't have to make me sit through all of your feelings for him. When you knew how much it would be hurting me. You *knew,* Sadie."

Sadie looked down once more. "I hoped you'd find a way around it," she said. Her voice grew quieter. "I had to talk to someone."

"Maybe you should have made more than one friend."

Daisy knew as she said the words that she would regret them later. But now, she felt nothing but a hot, sickly triumph as she turned and left Sadie staring at the floor.

***

"Emma Miller says she's going to be working with you next year."

Daisy almost laughed at the sound of consternation in her little sister Mary's voice.

"You can help too," she said.

"I don't want to dig in the dirt, I want to bake," said Mary, her expression indignant.

"Then what's the matter? Hold the lamp higher, would you?"

They were searching in the cellar for winter apples. Mary had been promised that she would be allowed to make an entire meal on her own from scratch, but Daisy had had to accompany her down to the dark cellar to find the ingredients. Mary had insisted that she was not scared, she was just being sensible. Going into the dark on your own was "just silly". Daisy had remembered Sadie saying something similar when they were small. She had wanted to laugh, and then wanted to cry.

"It's Sadie that's the matter," said Mary. "Did she do something?"

"Why do you ask that?"

"She hasn't been around. I thought maybe she did something."

Daisy was taken aback. Most people had assumed that Sadie had not been seen with Daisy because she was so caught up in her fledgling romance. Not that they had said as much, but Daisy could read raised eyebrows and conciliatory smiles as well as the next person.

"Why would she have done anything?"

Mary shrugged. "You're the nice one, everyone knows that."

Daisy flushed.

"Sadie is plenty nice," she said. "She just isn't as good at showing it. You have to get to know her."

Mary shrugged again, as though the whole thing didn't really matter. When they had enough apples, they headed back into the kitchen. Daisy was chased out by her sister. She donned her coat, and soon found herself treading the well-worn path down the back pasture to the wildflower meadow.

Was she, she wondered, the *nice one*? She made friends more easily that Sadie, true, but then she had been more than willing to throw that very fact in Sadie's face when they had fought.

But Sadie had hurt her, too. *He doesn't like you*, she'd reminded Daisy, as though she had needed reminding.

Maybe we're as bad as each other, she thought, as she reached the meadow. She stood at the edge and looked it over, an unpromising muddy patch of grasses and sticks. Nothing to be seen of its former loveliness. It just seemed like one more washed-out shade of gray in the uncompromisingly bleak winter landscape.

They had worked on this together. Spent hours at a time, carefully tending to each flower, careful not to do too much in case they smothered the plants with too much attention.

Everyone had warned them that they might grow tired of one another's company, working together each day as they did. But they had only grown closer. How could they both have been so willing to give it all up?

The edges of the nearby grass and bare stalks whipped in the wind, flicking against Daisy's dress. She leaned down and grabbed at a handful, pulling and twisting until the stems gave way.

What is left, she wondered, looking down at the dead things in her grip. *What is left of us?*

She heard someone clearing their throat, and turned toward the fence separating the meadow from the pasture.

And there he was. Isaac. Looking the same as he always did, his smile to one side, his eyes curious. But though Daisy felt her heart echo its old, familiar thump, the feeling was muffled and muted by sorrow. Isaac was no longer an ideal, but a reminder of her failures and losses.

"Checking up on things?" he asked, leaning his forearms on the fence.

Daisy glanced at the dim wilderness behind her. "Not much to see at this time of year," she said.

"I bet you're missing it, right?"

"I am."

"Sadie's missing it as well. I know she'll be excited when spring arrives."

Now Daisy's heart truly did ache. Sadie had not mentioned their falling out to Isaac, which she appreciated. But she was missing their work... was she missing Daisy as much as Daisy was missing her?

"She said so?"

Isaac shook his head. "She keeps talking about them, though, the flowers. More and more. I can tell that she's thinking about them all the time."

He smiled, and looked out across the dull expanse. "I know all the names of them by now. I'll be surprised if she doesn't start testing me on them soon."

Daisy laughed, despite herself, because that was so very like Sadie. "How many can you recite?"

"Uh... foxgloves," said Isaac, looking upward as though the answers were written on the clouds. "Poppies, bluebells, blanketflowers, sweet william, uh..." he glanced back down at Daisy. "Daisies."

"That's just cheating."

"Daisy's daisies," Isaac grinned. "Like it was meant to be. Sadie told me about that, you know, about when you two were born, both being called Sadie."

"That we were such good friends I gave her my name?" said Daisy, with a short laugh. Even as she felt a flicker of resentment, her mind was awash with shame over her pettiness. It was, really, such an absurd thing to get upset over.

"I guess," said Isaac. "Though she said sometimes she wishes it was the other way around, the naming."

"...Really?"

"Well, it's different, you know, it's unusual. Sadie's a pretty common name. She said she likes the idea of a flower name, that it goes with your nature and makes you sweet."

It was a lovely thing to say. The kind of thing that Daisy had always imagined Isaac would say to her on his own. But even if she could pretend that the words were his, and not Sadie's, Daisy realized that she did not want to. She did not want him. She could not.

"I bet *you* think Sadie's a pretty nice name?" she said, smiling.

Isaac laughed at this. Then his attention was caught by the stems still clutched in Daisy's hand.

"Are those dead?" he asked.

Daisy looked down at them – and then further down, to the place where she had pulled off the stems. She saw a tiny flash of soft, pale green.

"No," she said. "The roots are still there."

***

As well as Daisy knew the way from her home to the wildflower meadow, she knew the path to Sadie's home just as well. And after she said her goodbyes to Isaac, she found her feet following the trail without even thinking about it beforehand.

Through a small copse of trees, up a slight rise, over the fields and down a lane. Daisy took each step as though she were falling; she could not have held herself back, even as she feared where the journey would lead.

And when she walked in through the kitchen door and found Sadie, right where Daisy had known she would be, she still could not stop. She kept walking right up to her friend and wrapped her in a hug.

Sadie hesitated for only a moment before returning the embrace.

When they finally released one another, Daisy spoke first.

"I saw Isaac," she said. And then, "I'm sorry."

Sadie stared at her. "You mean... you don't love him anymore?"

Daisy could hear the hope in Sadie's voice, and wished that she could say yes with a clear heart. But she knew that it would take time to rid herself of the dreams she had let herself live in for so long.

"I love you more," she said. "So much more."

At this, Sadie shook her head. Her eyes dimmed with tears. "You love everyone," she said. "It's so easy for you. I'm not like that."

Daisy pushed her gently. "Don't be silly," she said. "You just have higher standards."

Sadie laughed a little. "It's true, though," she said. "You love everyone, and you're nice to them. All those little girls hang on your every word... I'm not like that. I never knew what to do, with those boys, suddenly wanting my attentions. I was offered love, and I didn't know what to do with it. I never did anything to deserve it, not like you."

"People think I'm nicer than I am," said Daisy.

Sadie's mouth twitched a little. "Well, that's probably true... but still. I never asked for anyone to like me, and I hated that you were overlooked. But with Isaac, it suddenly seemed to happen. And I'm sorry – I really am, so sorry. I'm not sure if I didn't realize how much he meant to you, or if I chose not to see it. I knew you liked him, but it was only afterward that I saw how much you hated all of it. But I couldn't bring myself to withdraw from either of you. I was selfish."

"...That's probably true." Daisy said, and the two friends shared a half smile. "But I understand."

"I hated hurting you," said Sadie. "I hated that he looked at me and not you, even though I was grateful at the same time. For the first time, really, I was grateful for... well. This."

She waved her hand vaguely in front of her face, to indicate the features that had ensnared to many hearts.

"It's not that," said Daisy, pushing her hand back down. "It might have been, a little, but it's not just that. The way he talks about you, the way he knows you – it's real. I can tell." She poked Sadie in the shoulder. "You're much easier to love that you think."

"Ha," said Sadie. She took a deep, shuddery breath, and something in the room seemed to relax.

Daisy drew a hand over her face and was surprised to find tears on her cheeks. Both girls looked away for a moment, composing themselves.

"I think we need tea," said Sadie. She put the kettle on the stove, then led the way to the table where they both sat down. After a moment, she looked at Daisy with another half smile. "Tell you what, you know who's easy to love?"

"I can guess," said Daisy drily. *Isaac.* Soon, she thought, she would be able to think of his name like anyone else's. She promised herself that she would.

"Maybe with you loving everyone, and him being so easy to find loveable, it was inevitable that you should care for him," sighed Sadie.

But Daisy had been thinking about this, as well.

"I don't know," she said slowly. It was painful to admit this, but she thought that if she could tell anyone, she could tell Sadie. "I think that my feelings for him were more to do with me. You know? I never thought about what would make him happy, just that I imagined he would make *me* happy."

Sadie nodded.

There was a pause. It was not completely comfortable, but Daisy felt that any pain present was the pain that came with healing. This process would take time. But, while they waited, they would have work to do.

"By the way," she said. "I was thinking about transplanting some zinnas from our back garden into the meadow this year. What do you think?"

Sadie's eyes immediately lit with interest, heartache and grief lost as plans and practicality rose to the surface.

"Yes," she said. "We've got some too, the cut-and-come-agains along the front fence. Maybe on the south side? Hold on, I'll get some paper."

"I'll make tea," said Daisy, heading for the stove.

"Oh – by the way – " Sadie hesitated in the doorway. "Why is little Emma Miller telling everyone that she's your apprentice?"

"Oh." Daisy brought a hand to her cheek. "Ah... I, well."

Sadie raised an eyebrow.

"...She caught me at a weak moment?" Daisy offered.

Sadie rolled her eyes and walked away, muttering about soft hearts and business sense.

Daisy grinned to herself, and went to fetch the teapot.

Susan's Rumspringa

SABRINA VICKS

Chapter 1

"Are you ready for tomorrow?" Susan's mother asked her as they sat together at the dining room table. Susan looked at her mother and twirled her cinnamon locks in between her fingers.

"I think so," she said nodding. "It's funny how you wait for this day to come for some many years and it seems so exciting, but now it has finally arrived and I am so nervous, I'm practically shaking."

"Rumspringa is a crucial time for the Amish youth, Susan. You will go out into the world beyond our community and you will get to experience and see things you have never thought were possible. It will be shocking, but it will also be fun for you." Susan's mother took her hand and gently brushed her fingers. "You have grown up so fast. It seems that it was only yesterday that you were a little girl, running in the fields and laughing with friends."

"Mother?" Susan asked, "Are you worried that I will choose to stay out there? Do you think I won't come back?"

Her mother smiled softly and shook her head, "Let's get some rest. Tomorrow will be a big day for both of us."

Susan went into her bedroom and closed the door behind her. She laid down in her bed and thoughts swirled in her mind about all of the possibilities the next couple of years might bring. She thought about the previous years and how she would watch parents saying goodbye to their children, but they almost always came back in the end. There were only a few times that she could think of where a person would decide to leave the church and try to make it out there in the world.

She could not understand what would compel a person to make that decision, but maybe she was about to find out.

***

Susan woke up in the morning earlier than usual. She could feel butterflies fluttering around her stomach as she sat up on her bed. She looked around the room and gave some quiet thanks for everything she'd been blessed with before standing up and getting dressed.

As she walked out of her room, she thought what a lovely surprise it would be for her mother if she made breakfast for her this morning. She made her way into the kitchen, and to her surprise, her mother was already in there stirring away.

"Mom?" Susan laughed, "You couldn't sleep either?"

"Not today! It's a big day for you and I wanted to make sure that you had enough food to keep you strong," her mother answered without looking up at Susan.

"It's alright, mom, it's only two years. It's not a lifetime!"

"Yes, well, let's pray that is the case." Her mother looked over her shoulder and flashed Susan a small smile. Susan went over to her side and the two of them finished preparing their meal in silence. As they sat down to take in their meal, they gave thanks to the Lord for His bounty and then began eating the last meal before Susan began her adventure.

Chapter 2

Susan followed the group of teenagers into the woods where they had prepared a party. She'd heard about these parties before—many of them ended with police getting involved somehow. She knew that she didn't want to spend all of her time here drinking beer, but she felt an obligation to try it at least once.

She stood at the edge of the clearing in the woods and watched all of her friends drinking and laughing and dancing. She sipped her own cup timidly, but soon the liquid sent a warm feeling over her and ironically, although she was outside, she felt that she needed fresh air.

She walked out of the woods by herself, surprised that it was so light outside still. The trees were so large and shady that she almost felt it was night. She walked along the road until she noticed a small shelter with a bench. She sat down on the bench and looked at the images around her. The one on the side of the wall of the shelter was a map with different color lines and pinpoints. Behind her with images of faces wearing too much makeup and announcing some sort of special dates.

Just then, she noticed a large vehicle driving down the road. It slowed to stop right before her and two doors automatically opened for her. The man who sat behind the wheel looked at her and said, "Hey, are you coming on or not?" Susan looked around to see if he could possibly be talking to anyone else, but there wasn't anyone else around.

She nodded and climbed up the large black steps leading inside of the vehicle. The bus driver looked her up and down and sighed audibly before shutting the doors behind her.

"I'm assuming you don't have any money to pay for this, do you?" The driver asked. Susan shook her head no and he just shrugged his shoulders and told her to take a seat in the back.

She walked towards the back of the bus, but before she found a seat, the driver took off and Susan lost her footing and fell into the seat where a young girl was sitting.

"Hey, watch out!" the girl shouted.

"I am so sorry," Susan apologized, "I wasn't prepared for the bus to move like that." The girl looked Susan up and down, obviously wondering about her long dress and bonnet. Instead of laughing at her or ignoring her, the girl smiled and patted the seat next to hers.

"Sit here," the girl said. She reached out her hand to Susan and introduced herself, "I'm Becky."

"It's wonderful to meet you, Becky," Susan smiled at her new friend, "I'm Susan."

"Cool," Becky said, "Where are you going?"

"Going?"

"Yeah, like, what stop are you getting off at?"

"I, uh, I'm not really sure exactly."

Becky looked at Susan and offered her a small rectangular device that lit up whenever she moved it.

"What is this?"

"Are you—what in the, where are you from? That's a cell phone. I thought you should probably call your parents or something and tell them that you're hanging out with me today!"

"Oh, that's very thoughtful. My mother knows I will be out for a while."

"Sounds good to me!" Becky clapped her hands together, "So, I was going to head to the mall. Do you want to come with me?"

"What's a mall?" Susan asked.

Becky smiled and responded, "Just stick with me, girl, and everything will be just fine."

Susan and Becky chatted with each other for the remainder of the bus ride with such ease, as if they had been long time friends. Susan told Becky about her life living in an Amish community and she explained the tradition of Rumspringa, which is why she was out experiencing the world.

"That is totally cool," Becky gushed, "I always thought that, like, you guys didn't really get a choice or anything."

"Not at all," Susan explained, "See we can't even get officially baptized in the church until we make the decision to do that. That's why we have this tradition so we can see how life is elsewhere and decide ultimately how we want to live."

"Do you know what you're going to decide?" Becky asked, but before Susan could respond, Becky yelled, "We're here! This is our stop. Come on!"

Susan climbed off the bus behind Becky and she stood on a busy street which faced a large glass building. The two girls made their way across the street and Susan found herself in a store surrounded by clothes—every style and color imaginable. She could not even fathom the idea of wearing some of things that she saw on the fake humans (mannequins, she heard Becky call them).

Becky grabbed a handful of different tops and jeans to try on and then headed to the back of the store where there was a fitting room. She put on each combination and then came out and paraded it around for Susan to judge whether or not she liked it. Of course, Susan didn't have much of an opinion on this type of fashion, so she would always say it looked great.

"Last one, Susan. What do you think?"

"Wow, Becky! I think that looks great!"

"It does, right?" Becky laughed, "Hey, I have an idea, you should totally try something on!"

Susan laughed, "No, I couldn't do that."

"Come on, come on, it will be fun. I promise!" Susan bit her lower lip debating whether or not she should try anything on. She felt like her mother would probably frown upon it, but at the same time, wasn't this the whole idea behind Rumspringa?

"Okay, I'll try on one thing," Susan decided. Becky clapped her hands in delight and handed her a pair of jeans that she had just tried herself. Susan went into the small room and closed the door behind her. She saw her reflection in the mirror as she undressed and she felt embarrassed by her own body. She quickly pulled her dress back on and slipped the jeans on under. Susan walked out of the room to show Becky.

"So?" Susan asked.

"Where are they?" Becky asked. Susan lifted the skirt of her dress slightly. "Wow, they look so good on you, Susan. You have to get them."

"I couldn't," Susan said feeling her cheeks getting hot.

"Let's go!" Becky said rushing them over to a small counter. She pushed all of her items towards a young woman standing on the other side.

"Will this be all?" the woman asked.

"Those too," Becky said pointing at the jeans Susan was wearing. She looked over at Susan with a huge smile on her face.

"Thank you, Becky. That is really very kind of you." Becky winked at Susan before handing over a small plastic card to take care of the transaction. Once Becky's items were folded into a small plastic bag, the two girls headed into the other side of the mall.

They walked side by side and Susan couldn't help but gawk at everything around her. The building was full of different stores selling so many things—clothes, electronics, furniture, baby things—she was starting to feel a bit overwhelmed by it all.

"And this," Becky said, stopping in front of a small booth with a curtain hanging over one side, "This is the real reason why I come to the mall."

"What is it?" Susan asked her.

"It's a machine that records you," Becky explained, "So it's like you sing karaoke, but it actually records you and makes an mp3 that you can take home!"

Susan just stared at her not even knowing where to begin with her questions.

"What?" Becky asked, noticeably disappointed in Susan's lack of a reaction, "You don't like singing?"

"Singing?" Susan repeated, "Oh, I sing every day with the choir. I love it! I just—well, I'm not sure, what is karaoke? And what is an mp3?"

Becky just laughed, "I'll show you. Let's go!" The two girls stepped inside of the machine and Susan watched as Becky inserted some money. The screen lit up and Becky scrolled through an endless list of song options. Finally, she selected an option and handed Susan a thing called a microphone. When Susan spoke into it, her voice was so much louder and she looked at Becky who just smiled.

The song started and it had a quick tempo. Susan watched words appear on the screen and suddenly, Becky started singing. Susan noticed that she sang whatever word came up and soon, Susan found herself nodding in time with the music. All too soon, the song ended and another screen popped up. Becky typed in something—she called it an email address—and explained that when she got home, she would be able to download the song and listen to it again.

Becky asked Susan if she wanted to try it, but Susan had no idea what any of these songs were, so she just shook her head. Becky did one more song and Susan wished that she was able to join in.

As the girls headed out from the mall, they waited at the bus stop together. Becky explained that they had to get on different buses now since Becky was heading home.

"Do you want to meet again tomorrow?" Becky asked, "We can try to do more songs!"

"Sure," Susan smiled, secretly wishing she could sing as well.

"Here," Becky said, handing her a small silver device. "This is called an iPod and it plays music. You just click this center button here, and put these in your ears, and the songs will play. Listen through them and tomorrow you can try one of these songs!"

Susan's eyes filled with small tears. She had known selflessness in her community, but for some reason, this kindness coming from this girl whom she just met struck her as being something amazing.

"Thank you, so much," Susan said. She boarded the next bus and waved at Becky as it pulled away from the bus stop. Following Becky's instructions, she rode the bus for about an hour before her stop. Once she got there, she walked the rest of the way back to the community.

She hid the iPod in her bonnet and made sure that her dress covered her new jeans completely. She couldn't believe that in one day, she experienced so much of the new world already.

She could only imagine how much more there was to learn.

Susan walked over to the side of the river and sat down beneath a shady tree. She pulled out the iPod and stuck the small white circles into her ears. Pressing the button, her ears were suddenly filled with the sounds of music. She sat there for a while, just listening as the various beats, melodies, and lyrics filled her head. Some songs Becky had even gave thanks to God, which made Susan smile.

Suddenly, she felt a tap on her shoulder. She jumped from her seat on the ground and ripped the earplugs out of her ear, struggling to hide it.

"Don't worry," the boy smiled, "I won't tell anyone."

Susan smiled appreciatively, "Thank you, Jacob." She tucked the iPod back under her bonnet and said, "It's Rumspringa. I met a nice girl and she let me borrow this device to listen to some songs."

"Do you like it?"

"Which? Rumspringa?"

"No, the music," he amended.

"Oh, yes," Susan gushed, "It really is quite catchy. But I do love the slower songs, some of the lyrics are beautiful."

Jacob nodded, understanding, "Yes, I remember. The music was one of my favorite parts of Rumspringa as well.

Can I tell you a secret?" Susan nodded. "I even though about leaving the community to try learning the drums!" Susan let out a quiet laugh.

"Oh, Jacob, you would never leave us," she said.

"No, I suppose that's why I ended up choosing the church after all," he smiled. "Can I walk you back home?" Susan nodded and the two of them walked together back to her house where her mother was waiting.

"So, have you thought about your decision? Do you know what you want to do yet?" Jacob asked.

"I think so," Susan said, smiling before walking up to the door of her house.

Jacob waved a final goodbye and walked away from the house as Susan pulled open the door and walked inside.

"Mother?" Susan called out, "Mother, I'm home!" She didn't hear a sound. Looking around the house, she finally found her mother curled up in her bed, asleep.

"Are you okay?" Susan rushed over to the side of her mother's bed and put the back of her hand to her mother's forehead.

Her mother mumbled something under her breath before pushing Susan's hand from her head.

"What did you say, mom? Are you feeling well?"

"I said," her mother was barely whispering and Susan had to lean forward to catch the rest of her words, "Please leave me alone."

Susan sat back on her heels. She debated her mother's words but she had never disobeyed her before. She left the room and pulled the door closed behind her. Susan could not even think of a time she ever saw her mother in bed before sundown, but she thought that perhaps she just wasn't feeling well and needed rest.

Susan went into her own room and pulled out the iPod again. She pushed in the ear plugs and pressed play, falling asleep to the new sounds washing over her.

Chapter 3

Susan woke up in the morning to loud clattering sounds coming from the kitchen. She got out of bed and pulled on her newly purchased jeans and pulled her dress over the top. She placed the iPod on top of her head and tied her bonnet securely in place, ensuring that nothing looked out of the ordinary.

She made her way into the kitchen to find her mother sitting at the table with her head in her hands.

"Mom?" Susan asked quietly. Her mother looked at Susan with a tear stained face. Her eyes were puffy and red. "Mom, what's wrong?"

Her mother shrugged her shoulders and smiled saying, "Nothing is wrong," she laughed, "I have no idea why I am crying. Just ignore me, Susie bug, I'm just a little out of it I suppose. Many things happening around here and you going on Rumspringa, I guess it's just hitting me."

"Do you want me to stay home today?" Susan asked.

"Don't be silly, Susan, of course that's not what I want. Go, go. Have fun!"

Susan smiled uncertainly at her mother but she stood from her seat anyways and headed towards the front door. Something was definitely going on with her mother—Susan could not even recall any time she'd ever seen her mother cry before. And she'd sent Susan out of the house without breakfast which she was certain had never happened in her 16 years of living.

She decided to try and leave it behind her as she left the community and walked towards the bus stop. Susan thought back to the directions that Becky had given her yesterday and waited for that specific bus. After about a ten-minute wait, the bus pulled up and Susan climbed on board. Becky was in the middle seats and waved at Susan as soon as her head appeared.

"No money again today?" the bus driver said. Susan looked at him and shrugged an apology, "I'm sorry but unless you have the bus fare, I can't let you on."

Susan looked back at Becky and said, "I'm sorry, Becky. He won't let me on unless I have the fare!" Becky jumped out of her seat and ran to the front of the bus plopping a few coins into a tall silver machine.

The bus driver looked at Susan and said, "You have a nice friend."

Susan nodded and replied, "I know." The two girls ventured further back in the bus and took their seats.

"So, did you get to listen to any of the songs on there?" Becky asked.

Susan nodded, "I actually fell asleep listening to all of your music! I love how different every song is and some of the lyrics are just incredible."

"I know, right?" Becky gushed, "Music is seriously my life. Do you know which song you want to try on karaoke today?"

"Does it let you record your own songs?" Susan asked.

Becky frowned, "No, it has to be one of the karaoke choices that are available. That's the only bad thing about this machine."

"Oh," Susan looked disappointed, "Well, I can watch you again today!"

"Wait a minute," Becky said, pulling out her phone, "I think I have an idea." Becky dialed a number quickly into her phone and pressed the call button. The volume was loud enough that Susan could hear when the woman answered on the other end. "Mom? Are you still home?" The woman mumbled something. "Okay, that's fine. I'm actually headed back to the house now instead of the mall." The woman responded with something and then the call ended.

Susan looked at Becky, curious to hear what the idea was that she looked so excited about.

"You've never heard of YouTube, right?" Becky asked. Susan shook her head no. "Well, prepare yourself for what I like to call a music-ation." Becky pulled out her phone and her ear plugs and offered one to Susan. After clicking and typing, a new screen opened and Susan watched a little spinning circle. She looked at Becky curiously.

Suddenly, her ears were filled with music and Susan was actually seeing the person singing. She watched in amazement at the small screen, truly appreciating the majesty of modern technology.

"This is amazing," she whispered to Becky.

"I know!" Becky laughed, "So, I think we should totally do it. Let's start our own YouTube channel! I have a webcam on my laptop at home and we can record ourselves singing random songs. It will be awesome!"

Susan couldn't help but smile at Becky. She wasn't confident in Becky's idea of them showing up on the other end of the screen, but Becky was so enthusiastic, it was hard not to catch on.

The girls watched video after video and Susan never ceased to be amazed by the various types of music from the slow, lyrical songs to the upbeat ones with funky dances. They all had one thing in common—they made Susan feel more alive than she had ever felt in her entire life.

The bus pulled to a stop and Becky announced that it was time for them to disembark. They shuffled off of the bus together and headed down the street towards Becky's house. Susan looked around at all of the houses—some were huge and had towering trees standing in the front areas of the house while others were a bit smaller, but still too big to be practical in any sense.

Becky walked up the driveway to one of the large houses and pulled out keys from her purse.

"Welcome to my home," Becky said, pushing the door open for Susan. The first thing Susan noticed was that everything was completely white—the floors were white; the walls were white and the furniture (except for a few pillows and blankets) were white.

"It's so..." Susan trailed off.

"Boring?" Becky laughed, "I know. But trust me, my room could not be any more different if I tried." Becky led the way upstairs and Susan couldn't help but wonder in the back of her mind what people do with all of this space.

Becky pulled open a door and Susan almost went into shock by the burst of color. Her walls were painted half hot pink, half orange. Becky had posters of different bands hanging all over her room and she had a bright purple comforter spread messily across her bed.

"This is my sanctuary," Becky said. She walked over to her small white desk and took a silver square from it. Becky walked Susan through exactly what they would do and how it would post to the internet. "It's really simple! I'll go first."

Susan watched as Becky turned on the camera and gave a small introduction of herself before starting the music in the background and singing her song. Once she was done, she uploaded the video to her YouTube channel.

"See?" Becky said to Susan, "Easy peasy! Now you go."

"I don't think I can, Becky. Besides, they don't even have my music on here."

"That's okay! You can sing acapella."

Susan hesitated a moment longer before finally agreeing to record a video. Becky clicked the button and pointed at Susan to begin.

Susan closed her eyes and called to her mind the melody and the words that brought her peace on so many occasions. She opened her mouth and the beautiful music began pouring out. She sang to no one—she sang to everyone. Music breathed a new life into her and it made her feel as though nothing could be wrong in the world.

Once she was finished, she opened her eyes and saw Becky sitting there with tears in her eyes.

"That was...beautiful," Becky choked out, "I had no idea you could sing that well." Susan smiled, not entirely comfortable with the attention but also pleased that Becky had enjoyed the song she chose.

The girls worked on their channel for the rest of the day, taking small breaks only to chat about the differences between their lives. Susan was starting to understand exactly how some people chose the modern world over the community. There just seemed to be so much more going on outside of her small community walls.

When Susan saw the time, she figured she should be heading back now to check on her mother. Becky gave her the bus directions and Susan smiled and hugged her tightly.

The two girls agreed to meet in the same place tomorrow.

Susan rode back in the bus by herself, listening to more songs from Becky's iPod. When she got to her stop, she hid it beneath her bonnet and walked towards the community. She reached her house and walked in not sure what to expect.

"Mother?" Susan called out.

"You're home early!" her mother cried out, appearing in the kitchen.

"I thought you would say I arrived late?" Susan asked.

"Nonsense, Susan. It's Rumspringa, it only happens once in your life. Anyways, how was your day?" Susan studied her mother carefully struck by the buzzing energy that surrounded her which was so different from yesterday when Susan had found her mother lying in bed and this morning when her mother had been in tears at the kitchen table.

"I had a great day," Susan decided to brush off the strangeness, especially because her mother looked to be in high spirits now. "I have made a friend and her name is Becky and we talk a lot about music."

"That's wonderful, Susan," her mother smiled at her and then walked into the kitchen. Susan offered her assistance, but her mother shooed her away and told her to get herself cleaned up.

Once Susan had finished washing up, she walked back into the kitchen and saw that the table was covered with food.

"Mother? Why is there so much food? Are we expecting company?"

"Oh, yes dear. Didn't I tell you? Jacob asked to join us for dinner tonight." Susan looked over at the table, even for three people this was too much food and it seemed almost wasteful to have prepared so much, but she let it go. There was a knock at the door and Susan walked over to open it and found Jacob standing there.

"Hello, Susan," he smiled.

"Jacob, please come in."

"How was your day today? Did you learn anything new?" he asked her, a mischievous gleam in his eye.

Susan smiled. She was tempted to tell him all about her YouTube channel, but hesitated and decided not to. She wasn't sure how Jacob would react if he'd found out that she had advertised herself and her talents to the world.

"Wow," Jacob said as he sat down at the table, "What a feast!"

"Well, it's a special occasion I think, isn't it? Anyways, it's not often that we have guests over the house. So, let's give our thanks to the Lord for blessing us with such bounty and let's eat the wonderful meal He has prepared through my hands." Susan's mother smiled at them both as she bowed her head and led them in grace.

Once they had finished, they begin passing around the plates. Susan asked, "What did you mean it was a special occasion, mom?"

Susan's mother looked up at Jacob and Susan saw him clear his throat nervously. He laughed, "Well, I wasn't expecting this all to happen so soon, but Susan, I just wanted to let you know that I have really grown fond of you and I hope that you feel the same way. I would like to spend more time with you if that's okay with you?"

Susan nearly choked on her food. She hadn't been prepared for this at all, especially not in front of her mother. They were both looking at her now, expecting her to answer, and she had no idea what to say.

"I'm quite sure Susan will say yes," her mother smiled at Jacob who started shifting in his chair uncomfortably. "Right, Susan?"

Susan recovered herself enough to respond, "Jacob, I would love to spend more time with you, but this is Rumspringa and as my mother said to me, it only happens once in a lifetime and—" Susan was cut short by the clattering sound at the end of the table. Her mother had pushed her own plate to the floor and stood up, looking extremely upset.

"How could you do this to me, Susan?" her mother started crying, "How?" She walked away from the table and went into her bedroom, slamming the door closed behind her.

Jacob looked at Susan with his eyebrows raised.

"I'm so sorry, Jacob!" Susan apologized, "I do not want you to think that I don't enjoy your company and of course, I would like to spend more time with you, it's just that, right now—" Jacob cut Susan off when he lightly touched her hand.

"I understand, Susan," he smiled, "I'm not upset at all. I enjoyed my time during Rumspringa and I would not want to take you away from that at all."

"Thank you so much for understanding," Susan smiled, slightly embarrassed now.

"Is your mother okay?" he asked.

"I'm not sure, Jacob. She has been acting strangely over the past two days. I found her yesterday in her bed before the sun had gone down and this morning she was in tears. She seemed perfectly fine tonight until just now. I'm not sure what could be wrong."

"Maybe she is just worried because you are gone," Jacob suggested.

"Maybe," Susan shrugged. They finished their meal and Susan led Jacob outside. They wished each other a good night and Susan cleaned the kitchen, picking up her mother's plate from the floor. She opened the door to her mother's room and found her asleep in her bed.

Susan knew that something was wrong, but she had no idea what it could be.

Chapter 4

For the following weeks, the routine was always the same. Susan would get up and meet Becky at the bus stop. They would go to Becky's house and record videos and post them on their YouTube channel. The two girls would read through the comments that people would leave—the majority of them were compliments though some people did not have pleasant things to say at all.

Becky told Susan that during the summers, she stayed with her dad at the other end of town and that's why she would have to take the bus to get over to her mom's house since her dad didn't allow her to bring her laptop. Susan felt a little guilty about the laptop, but she also secretly loved having someone who was showing here all of the wonderful things in the world.

Soon, Becky would be back at her mother's house for when school starts again. Susan wasn't sure what she would do then, but Becky suggested that Susan could follow her throughout school and they could say that she was shadowing Becky.

Susan quickly agreed to this plan because not only did it mean she would be able to maintain her YouTube channel and her friendship with Becky, but it also gave her the opportunity to explore education beyond 8th grade which excited her.

The first day of school came and Susan took the bus to Becky's house with no trouble. She laughed as she recalled her first day on the bus when she had no idea what it was and now she had become an expert at public transportation. Susan knocked on Becky's door and Becky's mother answered.

"You must be Susan," her mother smiled at her, "Becky has told me so much about you. Come in!" Becky was finishing getting dressed and she took about another 5 minutes before she came downstairs.

"Susan!" Becky yelled excitedly, "You'll never believe what my mother bought me for my first day back to school!"

"What is it?" Susan asked, laughing at Becky's crazy eyes.

"A car! Come look, come look!" Becky led Susan out to the garage and opened the door and revealed a small, blue car with two doors. "It's not brand new or anything, but still. I'm so excited. We get to drive to school in style," Becky laughed, "Come on, let's go!"

The two girls rode together in the car with the music blasting. Susan felt amazing—as if nothing in the world could stop her. She loved feeling so free. The car ride ended too quickly as they pulled up in the parking lot for the school. Becky parked and the two of them got out of the car.

"Hey!" Becky and Susan turned around to see a boy with ashy brown hair waving at them.

"Hi Robert," Becky smiled as the boy walked up to them.

"Nice wheels!" he gushed when he saw Becky's car.

"Thanks!" Becky shook her keys excitably. "This," she said directing her attention to Susan, "is my best friend Robert. Probably the coolest dude you'll ever meet."

"Hey," he said, extending his hand out to Susan, "It's really nice to finally meet you, Susan. I've watched all of your videos—you have got one stellar voice!"

Susan blushed as she shook his hand and said, "Thank you."

The three of them walked into the school together, Becky and Robert complaining about how much work they would have to do even though it was only the first day. Susan was almost overwhelmed by the number of students here—so many different types of people walking through the hallways, talking with their friends about what they did over the summer.

A peppy blonde girl walked up to them and said, "Hey guys! Did you already buy your tickets to the dance?"

Robert replied, "Come on, Penny. We haven't even gotten our schedules yet, let alone tickets to a dance."

"You have to go, Robert," the girl whose name was Penny smiled at him and brushed his arm gently, "It's the back to school dance."

Robert nodded and looked over at Susan, "The only way I'll go is if she goes with me."

"Me?" Susan asked, clearly not expecting that to come from his mouth. Robert nodded and smiled.

"Will you go with me to the dance?" Susan agreed to go with him and the three of them walked over to the table to purchase the tickets. Robert handed one ticket to Susan and told her, "Don't lose this." Susan saw Penny roll her eyes, obviously not pleased with how all of that played out.

The rest of the day went by in a blur and Susan was exhausted by the end. Becky asked if she wanted to come over, but Susan thought it would be better to go home and check on her mother.

The bus ride passed in a blur and Susan was back at the stop before she knew it. She got off and headed back to her community where Jacob was waiting.

"Hey Jacob. What's going on?"

Jacob looked a little upset, "Your mother isn't doing too well, it seems Susan. Today she started yelling at the other women and telling them all that they were being lazy and that the Lord was watching them."

Susan felt drained, but she knew she couldn't deny that her mother needed her. She walked home and found her mother already in her bed asleep. Jacob sat down with her on the front porch as Susan put her face in her hands.

"I can't leave her," Susan mumbled. She thought back to the day and how happy she'd felt. She thought about Robert and the way his hand had touched hers when he'd given her the dance ticket. She imagined dancing with him and a sad smile crossed her lips.

"What is it?" Jacob asked.

Susan looked at him and said, "As the days pass, I become more and more tempted to stay in the modern world. They have so much to offer, but with all of that comes a price. People lose their sense of real happiness because they start relying on material things to make them happy."

Jacob looked over at Susan and took her hand in his. He nodded at her to continue.

"I think I would be happy for a little while out there," Susan admitted, "But after a while, I would be searching for something else, never even realizing that all I ever needed was home."

"Are you saying what I think you are saying?" Jacob asked.

Susan looked up at him and smiled, "I'm saying that I am staying here."

My Amish Roots

Nicola Meyer

Chapter 1

Haylee lay in the darkness of her room staring out of the window at the moon that hung low in the sky, her only consort in her lonely life. Four years after meeting Jase, her heart was broken into a million pieces and scattered across the vast expanse of her own insignificant universe. Move on, they said, he's not worth it, they said, you deserve better. What did they know? None of her so called friends could ever imagine how she felt deep down and how utterly destroyed she was when she walked in on Jase in the arms of her best friend, Lucile. Of course the first thing both of them shouted when caught in the act was – it's not what you think!

After Jase pleaded with her and Lucile convinced her that it was an irresponsible judgement error on her part and that it would never happen again, she gave it another shot. She should have known better. Naïve little Haylee, who only tries to see the good in people ended up as the biggest fool of them all and when it happened a second time, she could no longer be ignorant. It was obvious that between the chemical combination of Lucile's raging pheromones and Jase's ego boosted testosterone, she never stood a chance. She had to finally admit to herself that she was never going to find true love, and friendships are feeble pastimes for pre-schoolers.

It's been almost two months since her relationship with Jase ended, and it wasn't long after that, that she also handed in her resignation as an article clerk. Breaking up with Jase and seeing him once in a blue moon she could handle well, but working with him and sharing the same open office day in and day out was a little too much to handle. It amazed her how men in could be so callous and move on without a worry in the world. She had managed thus far, but the more she sat at home she started to feel cooped up like a bird in a too small cage.

She sighed and tugged her blanket over her shoulders and tucked it under her chin as she turned onto her other side, this time staring at her graduation photo. She stood tall and proud, alone in her toga with her rolled up certificate in her hand, no immediate family to share her successes with her. Her adoptive mother had passed away six months short of her graduation that year. Haylee sniffed and blinked away the tears. She didn't cry then and she won't cry now. Finally giving up on sleeping she tossed the blanket back and sat up in bed. Her mom always told her, that every person has left something behind in their past, that sits there and waits until they go back to find it and resolve it. And until recently she had never thought she wanted to go back there. She was only four when she was adopted, a lonely gray mouse stuck in foster care. From the first day she arrived at her new family, she was accepted and spoiled rotten. She never needed for anything in her life, and she never felt as if she was any different to any of the other kids, so why she suddenly felt like digging out the past was a mystery to her, but every day it became more and more pressing. And here at two in the morning, she was stuck between forcing herself to sleep or logging into her email to see if the adoption agency managed to track down her biological mother or family. Insomnia won the battle and she finally made herself a cup of coffee and sat down at her desk and logged into her emails.

Dear Miss Jones

We have managed to track down your biological mother, but it is with regret that we inform you that she passed away a few years ago due to illness. We have however managed to track down her parents, your grandparents. We do however wish that you consider the fact that they may not...

Hayley stared at the email, reading it over and over again, somehow grief evaded her, and it was like reading the sad story of a stranger. What she did learn from this was that her mother was born Amish, and that her grandparents lived in an Amish community in Ethridge, Tennessee. But even if she knew who they were, what good would that do now? It wasn't as if she could reunite with her long lost mother anymore. But what she might be able to figure out is what type of woman her mother was and what type of life she lived. Maybe it will even shed some light on why her mother gave her up for adoption. As she spent her time reading up on the Amish and their culture, it became more and more evident that her mother may not have had a choice, but this was pure speculation. And unless she took the time to find these things out for herself, she would always be guessing about the woman who brought her into this world.

Besides, it wasn't as if she had anything better to do with her time. She had no job, no love life and no coffee, she thought as she looked at the empty canister in front of her.

That was it; she was going to take the last of her savings and head to Ethridge and find the Lapp's.

Chapter 2

The whole way to Ethridge, Hayley kept wondering if she was making a mistake. She was about to embark on a journey she was in the least bit prepared for. Before she left everything behind, she made effort to reinvent her wardrobe with a few modest outfits just so that she wouldn't look too outrageous amongst the Amish. But even now as she sat in the back of the cab, her heart was beating a million miles a second and she was on the verge of having a nervous breakdown. She had just left behind the only life she knew, not that there was much left of her for her to salvage, but she was somewhat comfortable where she was.

The cab pulled into the small town of Ethridge and stopped in front of what appeared to be a touring business.

"This is as far as I can go," the cab driver said and pointed to this meter.

Hayley nodded and fished for cash to pay the cab driver and the moment her bags were offloaded and she stood like a singled out deer in hunting season outside on the sidewalk she wanted to burst out in tears. Whatever was she thinking coming out here?

"Hello, may I help you?"

Startled Hayley nearly lost her balance as she spun to look at the stranger behind her, "Oh-I-um, well, I'm looking for someone," she said and dug in her purse, "Mr. and Mrs. Lapp?"

"Oh Fredrick and Mary Lapp, yah, they live here. I can take you," the young man said.

"You know them?" Hayley asked in disbelief.

"Yah, well it's a small community we all know each other," he said tucking his thumbs under his suspenders.

Hayley couldn't help but stare, wondering if all Amish men were this good looking. This guy couldn't be much older than her twenty-five. And although he was dressed modestly in what she had to assume Amish clothes, he looked reasonably attractive. He had ebony black hair with willow green eyes set deeply in his skull.

"If you're done staring..." he said interrupting her thoughts with his brows drawn together.

Embarrassingly she shook her head, "I'm so sorry, I just... it has been a really long day and I've traveled a long way."

"No matter, my name is Duncan," he said and nodded his head courteously, extending his hand.

"Hayley," she said and gave his hand an overly firm shake.

"Well I best be getting you to the Lapp's, the weather is turning foul."

Without notice he started loading her luggage into a carriage that stood nearby and then patted the back of the carriage, indicating her seat.

Who was she to ask questions, she hadn't the foggiest about their customs and every website she visited to learn about them were know-it-all windbags who have made up assumptions. So instead of opposing she hopped into the back of the carriage and sat down.

"So do you know the Lapps?" Duncan called over his shoulder as they made their way into the town.

"I...sort of, actually, I knew their daughter," she lied, she had no clue what their daughter was like. Just because Hannah Lapp gave birth to her, didn't exactly mean she knew her.

"I think you might have them mistaken for someone different, they only have a son, but Kendrick moved to Lancaster with his wife."

Well, this was a good start, she thought as she tucked her lip under her teeth, "Perhaps I am confused, but I suppose there is no harm in meeting them. Maybe they might know Hannah Lapp as extended family."

"Hannah Lapp," Duncan repeated, "The name sounds familiar."

The carriage came to a halt and Hayley fell forward along with her luggage and just then the heavens opened up.

"Come!" Duncan called and reached for a sheet to cover her luggage before effortlessly lifting her off the wagon and placing her on her feet, "The Lapp's live here. If you hurry I can wait and take you back to Richland Inn."

"Wait, what do you mean back to town, I need to be here in Ethridge," she protested as Duncan lead her up to the house where the Lapps lived.

"Well if the Lapps won't let you stay in their home, you have nowhere else to stay, unless you want to sleep in the barn."

"The barn?" she asked appalled.

"Duncan, vas in der velt?" an elderly man interrupted as he opened his door.

Duncan immediately removed his hat and clutched it in front of him then looked at her before turning his attention back to the older man.

"Mister Lapp, this is Hayley. She's come to Ethridge to look for..."

Before Duncan could continue Hayley stepped up and extended her hand, "Grandfather?"

The older man's complexion paled, and he exchanged looks with Duncan then looked at Hayley, "You're mistaken," he mumbled and moved to close the door, but then an elderly woman appeared and the expression on her face was one of pure shock.

"Hannah... you look just like her," she said in a trembling voice as her eyes shot full of tears.

"Grandmother?" Haylee said as she stood with her hands folded in front of her.

"Come, you're going to get soaking wet out in the rain," she said as she dragged Hayley into the house, despite her Grandfather's disapproval.

And as she disappeared into the kitchen she heard her grandfather mumble for Duncan to bring her luggage inside.

Her grandparents, she couldn't believe it. She was actually in the very house her biological mother grew up in. Her grandmother seemed far more accepting of her than her grandfather did, but she refused to make any assumptions until she had all the facts. For now, she will take the time she had to get to know them.

Chapter 3

A week since her arrival and all she could determine was that her mother, Hanna Lapp went on a Rumspringa and never returned.

"Did she never write to you?" Hayley asked her grandmother one morning after her grandfather left to go to work.

"She wrote to us, but only ever to let us know she was fine," her grandmother said softly as she continued with her sewing.

"But weren't you in the least bit worried?"

Mary put down her sewing and reached out for Hayley's hand, "Yah, we were worried, especially your grandfather, but our laws are different to those on the outside. Hannah made her choice and she had a chance to return."

Hayley sat quietly for a moment and squeezed her grandmother's hand. The short while she had been here in the Amish community of Ethridge, she had found a sense of peace and tranquillity she never felt before. With the exception of a minority of locals who walked wide circles around her, the younger people like her were friendly and very accommodating. She couldn't understand why her mother would have left for good, and trade this life for what lay outside in the world. But then, being on holiday in a strange place was far different that living the life in full.

A knock on the door drew her attention and her grandmother quickly set her sewing aside and went to open the door, and a few seconds later she returned with Duncan in tow.

"Hayley, Duncan is here to see you," her grandmother said smiling.

Duncan was another person she was growing fond of at an alarming rate, but thankfully the walls she erected around herself kept her level headed. She knew that the only reason she felt closer to him than any of the others was that he was the first person she met when she arrived.

"Hi Duncan, what a nice surprise," she said standing up.

"Good day to you Hayley," he nodded tucking his thumbs in his suspenders, "I was wondering if you would like to go to the market today, I have a few errands to run."

Hayley felt the slight flutter of butterflies in her stomach and tugged her hand into her midriff. It would be rather nice to get out a little and get to know other parts of the community, she thought and then nodded.

"It would be lovely, let me get my coat and purse," she said and hurried to her room.

She forced herself not to eavesdrop on her grandmother' and Duncan's conversation and quickly got what she needed before joining them.

In no time they were on the carriage and on their way to the market, this time Hayley got to sit in the front and not like some baggage on the back.

"So how are you enjoying your stay here in Ethridge?" Duncan asked curiously.

"It's nice. I mean, it's very different to city life, but so far I'm enjoying the peace and quiet," she said and glanced out over the landscape.

"Yah, it's very quiet. So did you manage to find out about Hannah?"

"A little," she said.

She didn't want to put the Lapps in any sort of disrepute, but she found it hard to believe that Duncan had no clue about her, but then again, he was probably still a baby when Hannah left the Amish community.

"So will you be moving on then?" he said clearing his throat.

Hayley turned to look at him and smiled, "Not sure, maybe. Tell me about this Rumspringa thing."

Duncan laughed and looked at her, "Well, Rumspringa means to run around, when the youngsters turn sixteen they can choose to go out and experience things outside of our community. It's each one's choice, some do it and some don't."

"Did you ever, I mean did you do it when you turned sixteen?" she asked curiously.

"Nay, I never did. I have all I need right here."

"So you never wonder what lies out in the cities."

Duncan drew the carriage to a halt and then turned to look at Hayley, studying her with those intense willow green eyes.

"Most young men leave because they are not satisfied with their life here, mostly because they are tempted by the modern world, and women," he said, his cheeks growing rosy.

Hayley tried to hide her smile and coughed softly, "So you never wanted to go find some hanky-panky?"

"Hanky -panky?" Duncan asked and blinked, "What is that?"

"Uh... well meeting women, dating and so on."

Duncan threw his head back and laughed, "Oh no, I had no interest in those things. Not then anyway," he said and then tugged on the reins sending the horse back onto the road, "I always believed that at the right time God will send the right woman my way. I'm a patient man Hayley Jones."

When he looked at her then, she felt her heart flutter in her chest and she immediately looked the other way. Her mind was clearly playing tricks on her; there was no way that Duncan would even consider looking at her twice. She was an outsider for one, and secondly, she wasn't exactly a virgin either. And although she still knew very little about their laws and traditions, she was sure the Amish probably had the highest moral values in the world second to nuns.

The rest of their trip was in silence, and a few miles further they finally reached the Amish Country Mall. Hayley was quite surprised by the variety of goods that were sold at this place, but more so how many non-Amish visited the place. It was a tourist distraction for curious people. And as she stood next to Duncan and the Carriage in her own authentic Amish dress, a sense of pride washed over her. Surprised that she actually felt Amish in some far-fetched way, she smiled at Duncan and then headed into the shop. She found it quite amusing that it was called a Mall when all it really had were old antique trinkets and a limited menu of food. There were some items for sale but it was hardly considered anything close to a shopping mall. When she exited the store she found Duncan standing next to her grandfather, both in deep conversation. Instead of barging in on them she took a walk around the store to give them their own time. Her grandfather had hardly spoken a word to her since her arrival and he was still a great big mystery to her. On occasion when she did ask her gran about him, she simply avoided the topic. She wasn't any closer to find out exactly why her mother never came back.

Chapter 4

Duncan couldn't help but admire Hayley, and although she was an outsider, she seemed to adapt quite well to the Amish life. It's been two weeks since he met her, and the more time he spent with her the more he started to like her. The first day he saw her was the first time he ever really looked at a woman. She was modestly dressed in a floral print dress that flowed elegantly down her body to her calves, but what intrigued him most was her shyness. The fact that he had the impulsive need to run his fingers through her long brown tresses was abnormal for him and he quickly stifled that need, by reminding himself that she was an outsider, which helped.

Normally when outsiders visited the Amish communities they stuck to their modern clothes, where the women wore as little as possible. No wonder so many of the Amish boys opted to go on their expedition to the cities, being tempted by the promises that the modern world presented. Two of his own best friends went out to experience the world and all it had to offer, but he never felt that desire or pull to know what happens out there. He was more than content to live this life of simplicity, working on the farm and making goat's cheese. There were many times when he attended the sings and where he contemplated the option of taking a wife, but none of the girls here in Ethridge ever made him feel the way he did now. And he was adamant that if he was going to take a wife, it would be someone who would completely consume his thoughts. He wanted the same love with a wife than his mother and father shared. He had never seen them argue, and they always showed their affection towards each other. And if they could have such a devoted marriage, why could he not have the same?

Duncan was caught in his own thoughts when the smell of burning wood and grass wafted through the air.

"Duncan!" It was Hayley who rode towards him on one of the Lapp's horses, her eyes wide, "Come quick, my grandfather's barn is on fire!" she cried.

In an instant, Duncan had called his father and his neighbors, and everyone else he could alert and they were on their way by carriage to the Lapp's farmlands. Up ahead he could see the plume of fire explode into the gray sky. Flames rolled outwards and embers were flying up into the sky.

When he pulled up next to Hayley where she dismounted the horse, he took the reins and handed it to another young man, "Take the horse to my father's barn and keep it there," he instructed and then turned to Hayley, "What happened?"

"I have no idea, we were all having dinner when we heard the loud crash of lightning, and not long after that the smoke was everywhere," she said ringing her hands together.

Duncan's concern for Hayley had to be set aside, and although he wanted to comfort her, he had to attend to the bigger problem.

"Okay, go to the house and stay inside," he ordered as he scooped a bucket of water from the trough.

"But I can help," she protested and reached for a small barrel.

"You've done enough, now go and sit with your grandmother, I'm sure she could use the company."

Her mouth opened in protest but then shut, and with a slight nod, she ran across the field towards the house.

They fought all night to get the fire under control, thankfully the Lord had blessed them with rain to help put the fire out, but all that was left were the charred remains of the barn in the smoky morning air that reeked of burnt wood and straw. His father had warned Fredrick about the tall dead tree that stood so close to the barn. But misfortune led to lighting striking the dead tree and causing it to fall on to the barn. Luckily it was only the barn that burned down, somehow the horses were freed before the barn was completely on fire, and he has the slightest suspicion that it was Hayley's quick thinking that saved the animals. As for the equipment, it was all replaceable.

"Thank you, son, if you didn't arrive when you did I would have lost all my horses," Mr. Lapp said as he came to stand next to Duncan.

"Nay, that was not my doing. Hayley saved the horses," he said and looked at the older man.

"Hayley saved them?" he asked disbelievingly.

"Yah, she came to fetch me on horseback, I've never seen a woman ride so well, but she came to call me straight away. By the time I got here the horses were already in the fields and Kent took them to my barn."

Fredrick stood quietly for a while rubbing his chin, and Duncan knew that he had his own demons to face. He too had never heard of Hannah Lapp, but spending time with Hayley he had learned a great deal.

"She's seeking your approval," Duncan said crossing his arms as both of them looked at what remained of the barn, "She deserves a fair chance."

"You're right," Fredrick said and then headed towards the house.

Duncan looked as the older man walked away, his shoulders hunched as if he carried a heavy burden, but he knew Hayley deserved a fair chance, she had nothing to do with her mother's disobedience or her choice to give her up for adoption.

Later that day, Duncan stood in his father's barn, grooming the Lapps' horses. The least he could do was make sure that none of them were injured. But more than anything he needed to keep busy so that he could chase the thoughts of Hayley from his mind. Every waking hour was seemingly consumed by thoughts of her, and after her courageous act it was even worse. Now he knew exactly how King Solomon must have felt, being tempted by a beautiful woman.

"Duncan?" he heard Hayley's voice from outside the barn.

"In here!" he answered and tossed the brush in the sack hanging on the wall.

"Oh there you are," she said smiling and held out a basket for him, "Grandma and I baked these to thank you for helping us out with the horses."

Duncan smiled and took the basket filled with cookies, "Thanks, but I think you deserve all the credit, if it wasn't for you these horses would be charred with the barn."

He noticed Hayley blush as she averted her eyes, "I love horses, I had to do something."

Duncan stepped closer and reached out to tuck his finger under her chin, "And you did an amazing job of saving them," he said but his voice betrayed him.

This close to her, he could smell the fresh scent of lavender and vanilla, and although it was just the crook of his finger brushing her unblemished skin under her chin, it was the silk soft smoothness that tempted him more than anything. And without a second thought, he stepped in and pressed his lips against hers. Hers were soft, like cotton pillows and although the kiss was brief, it was a defying moment for him. He knew there and then that Hayley was the woman he'd been waiting for all these years.

He broke the chaste kiss but didn't step away from her; instead he kept his eyes locked on hers. It was that moment between two people where words were irrelevant syllables and consonants were fleeting sounds that would never be able to express the emotions that sparked between them.

It was Hayley that stepped away first, and how shyly tucked a strand of hair behind her ear.

"My grandfather said that they will be doing a barn rising this coming weekend, will you come?" she asked softly.

"I wouldn't miss it for the world," Duncan said.

And as Hayley walked back out of the Barn she looked back over at him again and smiled.

Duncan felt like a teenager for the first time, and now more than ever was he determined to make Hayley Jones his wife.

Chapter 5

The barn raising was well on its way, the men from the community had spent most of the morning working and Hayley was amazed by how quickly the barn started taking shape. She heard many stories about this experience and how the Amish are able to build an entire barn in one day, but she had never seen it with her own eyes. Duncan was at the front line of everything. He did the planning and the design, his skill as a builder came in handy and it appeared that young to old admired him, but not nearly as much as she did.

When she first decided to come to Ethridge, finding love was the last thing she anticipated. After her failed engagement to Jase, she had sworn off on ever dating again, but here she was, utterly captivated by Duncan. He was the complete opposite to Jase. He was kind, considerate, a true gentleman and there was something about him that she craved.

"He's a fine young man," her gran said as she handed her the basket of fresh fruit.

Hayley tore her eyes away from the barn and smiled at her gran, "Yes, he is," she admitted.

"You know, Hannah never told us about you until after she gave you up for adoption," her grandmother started, "When she told us your grandfather begged her to withdraw the adoption and rather send you to us."

Hayley sat down opposite her gran at the wooden table, "So you did know about me?"

"Oh yes we did, but your mother had already handed you to your new parents, and we had no way of finding you. That day you arrived here in Ethridge, you were a spitting image of my Hannah."

Hayley's eyes shot full of tears and she reached out to take her grandmother's hand, "My adopted parents were good people, they really looked after me as if I was their own."

"I know, but I can't help wonder just how things would have been if Hannah had come back home," the older woman admitted and lowered her eyes.

"I'm here now though, and you've made me feel at home."

"Yah, yah, I know. I've been trying my best. Your grandfather blames himself for what happened, but he's a good man."

Hayley smiled and then looked back at the men toiling in the sun. Her grandfather was a proud but humble man, and she knew that deep down he cared for her.

By six o'clock that evening, the barn stood tall in all its glory. Brand spanking new as if no disaster had struck it just a week ago, and everyone in the community had gathered to celebrate the event. It was a festive atmosphere and for the first time in her life Hayley felt as if she belonged. Over the weeks she spent here in Ethridge learning to bake and quilt, she hardly thought of her life in the city. And the hustle and bustle of peak hour traffic and busy shopping malls were nothing but a distant memory of a temporary life she once knew.

She made a few friends and even the older people had started to like her. Maybe it was due to the fact that she did not come here to dispute their faith or their ways, but she embraced it like any Amish citizen would.

From across the group of people, she caught Duncan looking at her. But instead of looking away, she smiled at him, and even when one of his friends tapped him on his shoulder he still looked her way, refusing to drop his glance. The sight of him made her knees weak. She had to force herself to look away before her grandfather came to sit beside her.

"My dear," he started sounding uncomfortable, "I owe you an apology for my behavior."

Hayley turned to her grandfather and smiled, "No need, you had a lot to cope with, with my untimely arrival. I should have taken better care to notify you before I just dropped in."

"No, it's not that. I-I never gave your mother a chance to rectify things and for that, I am forever guilty, I should have gone to find her."

Fredrick pinched the bridge of his nose and shut his eyes and Hayley knew he was fighting back the tears, she gently placed her hand on his, "The choices we make are our own, and we are all responsible for them, no one can take responsibility for the mistakes of others."

There was a moment of silence, and when her grandfather looked up at her again he smiled tenderly, "You will make a wonderful Amish woman," he said and patted her hand, "And Duncan would choose well to ask for your hand."

"Hayley, come!" One of the girls called and tugged her up by her hand, "You must join in on the sing."

Before Hayley could process the words of her grandfather she was caught smack bang in the middle with a bunch of the younger people, and although there were no instruments, the clapping of hands and the harmonies of voices made the songs come to life. Among the crowd was Duncan, subtly making his way closer to her and the closer he came the more her heart beat out of control and the butterflies that hijacked her insides fluttered up a storm. She might very well be an outsider but she could not deny the fact that somehow Providence had claimed a victory.

"Would you spare me a few minutes of your time?" Duncan whispered as he reached her.

"Of course," she said and followed him outside.

Duncan had his hands tucked in his pockets as he stood outside. The moonlight spilled down from the heavens like a silver curtain, bathing their surroundings in silver dust and casting its subtle glow over them. And as Hayley came to stand next to him, they both glanced up at the sky.

"Hayley..."

"Duncan..."

They started at the same time and then burst out laughing.

"You first," Hayley insisted and Duncan smiled and turned towards her.

"Okay, well, I'm sure this will come as no surprise to you, but I thought it best I clear the air," he started clutching his hand in his hands, "I think or rather, I know that I have grown very fond of you, and I know that it may be a little more complicated than usual, but I have spoken to your grandfather."

Hayley stood playing with the string of her prayer cap, coiling it around her index finger nervously. It felt as if her heart was going to jump out of her throat as Duncan went on, explaining how he had asked her grandfather if he would allow him to court her. A few weeks ago, she would never have considered this, but now where she stood under the moonlit sky, with her hand in Duncan's she knew exactly what she wanted.

"And did my grandfather approve?" she asked curiously biting her lip.

"He did indeed, which is why I have gathered to courage to ask you in person," he admitted and smiled.

Hayley shifted her weight and sucked in a breath, she had no idea how Amish dating customs worked. Of all the things she had yet to learn, dating hardly featured and she recalled only briefly spot reading over that section.

"So are we going to be bundling?" she asked innocently and blushed.

Duncan raised his brows and chuckled, "My dear Hayley, you have so much to learn still, no one does that anymore," he said and stepped closer to her and reached to remove her prayer cap.

"Is that allowed?" She whispered softly as Duncan's lips hovered over hers and he pulled the pin that secured her hair in a bun lose.

"What happens between us, and the Lord, is all that matters," he said and then wrapped her loose braid around his hand and kissed her fully on the lips.

Chapter 6

Hayley stood in front of the mirror, while her grandmother fussed with her long hair. It's been a year since she joined the community and although her and Duncan's feelings for each other were no secret to the rest of the community, they both kept their word to follow the rules and customs as required by the Amish Council.

"So the food is almost ready. Once your Grandfather and I are off to the church service, you and Duncan can sit down and celebrate your betrothal."

Hayley looked in the reflection of the mirror at her grandmother, the woman she had grown to love and smiled, "Do you think I will make him happy, Grossmammi?" she asked.

"Natuurlijk! You're his future and the woman he had been waiting for all this time," her gran reassured her.

After her grandparents left to go to church, where the minister would be announcing the brides to be, she waited patiently at the house for Duncan to arrive. She kept looking at the clock on the wall, it was a unique hand crafted clock made especially for her by Duncan, as a courtship gift. Time seemed like it had deliberately slowed down, and when she heard the carriage finally pull up in front of the house, she had to force herself to stay calm and not rush into his arms. Other than the first time he kissed her, and the second and the third, this was probably one of the most amazing moments in her life. After tonight, she would officially be engaged, and by October, only two months away, she would be Mrs. Hayley Beiler.

"You do know that you still have a choice right?" Duncan said much later after they had finished dessert.

"I have made my choice, and it is to stay here with you," she said smiling.

They were seated on a wooden bench outside on the porch; waiting for the Lapp's to arrive.

"Are you a hundred percent sure?" he asked again, this time lacing his fingers with hers.

Hayley turned to him and placed her free hand over their entwined fingers. The past few months she had made the effort to learn their various customs, do bible study, get familiar with their laws, but she knew beyond anything that her life was here with him.

"Duncan, I am happy and I would not change this for anything," she said and then leaned close enough for her lips to brush his, "Ich liebe dich," she whispered and gave him a chaste kiss on his lips.

"And I love you, Hayley Jones," Duncan said, smiling from ear to ear and then quoted Songs of Solomon, "You are altogether beautiful, my darling, beautiful in every way."

~*~

Most of all, let love guide your way. Col 3:14

AMISH CREEK
MONICA MARKS

<u>**Winter**</u>

The night had taken on a cold chill and it was somehow fitting of the heaviness in Jacob's heart. He gently urged the horses forward as they shied from an oncoming car, carefully guiding them closer to the ditch at the side of the road. Ahead of his carriage were two more, one for each of his brothers and their respective wives. The family was approaching the market and Jacob was grateful for his hands were slowly freezing against the reins despite the heavy woolen gloves covering them. The three carts eased into the wide parking area to the left of the treeline and Eliza, Jacob's younger sister-in-law, was the first out of carriage, already busying herself with the merchandise in the back of the wagon. By the time Jacob pulled his horses to a full stop, she had managed to unload a substantial number of goods. She smiled briefly at him as he approached to assist her but waved him away.

"It's all right, Jacob, I am quite capable of handling this here. You can go about whatever you need to do in your carriage." Jacob nodded but said nothing. He had never been one to say much.

"That's why you're not married," Jonah would tease him. "The women have no idea what you're thinking. How are they supposed to know that you have marriage on your mind when you say so little?" Jonah had no way of knowing how his words upset Jacob as it was merely meant to be brotherly teasing but Jacob often wished that he was more outspoken. Yet when he was in the presence of his female peers, he found himself more tongue-tied than usual. Gabriel and Jonah often pointed out the blue painted gates of the eligible women in town but Jacob always averted his eyes and changed the subject or maintained complete silence. Eliza and Jonah had just wed the previous month and as his just barely younger brother hopped down to join his new wife, Jacob could not help but feel a pang of envy at the new scruff covering his sibling's face. Subconsciously, Jacob found himself touching his own clean shaven, soft cheek, wondering if he would ever be able to boast the beard of a married man.

"Come along now, Jacob," Gabriel urged suddenly appearing at his side. "The cheese will freeze if you stand here too long."

"Really, Jacob," Louisa scowled. "You know better than to stand there while our goods go bad." At the sound of his older sister-in-law's voice, Jacob shifted his eyes downward and picked up the pace of unpacking the freshly churned cheese onto the wheelbarrows Eliza had dug out from the depth of her cart. Louisa was the dark, complete opposite of Jonah's sweet natured, cheerful mate. Louisa was only a year older than Jacob but she looked and acted like Jacob's ninety-year-old grandmother. She was starch and rigid and unlike Jacob's beloved grandmother, never had a kind word to say. Jacob could never understand why his older brother, Gabriel had married such an embittered woman. Gabriel was without a doubt the most attractive and hardest working member of their family. He was mild mannered and intelligent and he could have had his pick of any number of eligible women in their community. However, that was neither here nor there at that moment as Louisa's look of anger was deepening by the second as she watched Jacob's idling. Gabriel took the wheelbarrow from Jacob's hands, also noticing the look on Louisa's face and followed Jonah and Eliza toward the indoor market, Jacob close behind them, Louisa on his heels like a rabid sheepdog trying to keep in in line. Once inside, Jacob was relieved for the wood burning stoves which were filled with fresh wood and already warming the giant barn, despite the early morning hour. Someone had taken care to ensure the vendors were comfortable upon their arrival. It was barely six o'clock and the winter sun had yet to break through the blackness of night but the smell of the wood against cold winter air brought a surge of familiar melancholy to Jacob. He had been feeling lost the past few months, as if he were missing a key element, like air or water. He suspected that Jonah's wedding had helped bring about the sudden loneliness. *You need to find a wife and start a family. You're twenty-five years old. You are the last man in the family and you're unmarried. Even your younger brother is married before you! That is shameful!* Louisa's sharp tone snapped him out of his brooding.

"Are you going to stand there until the sun goes down, Jacob?" He shuffled forward without looking up, joining the rest of his family at their booth. He liked this venue. It was a true Amish market, lit with soft gaslights and no electricity. It had once been an old, neglected barn belonging to a vast colonial house but years after the family who had owned it went bankrupt, the land was distributed among the Amish communities evenly. The house had been demolished and Jacob's family lived on one part of the fruitful farmland, raising goats, cows and chickens. They had been dairy farmers for generations. A neighboring district had reconstructed the dilapidated barn, expanding it to four times its size and they had created a small trader's market within the grand structure. Everyone was welcome, provided they respected the land. On any given day from Tuesday to Saturday, there were merchants selling jams and quilts, sweaters and meats. Only the freshest vegetables and cheeses could be found in the simple wooden booths, packed in ice and metal buckets. Once in a while, a more ambitious traveler would set up a crate boasting homemade wine or cider but those peddlers were becoming more and more scarce as the demand for their supply diminished. While it was open to the general public, it maintained the virtue in which Jacob was raised and he felt more at home at this particular location than any of the others at which they frequented over the year. Their cheeses were on display in a very short time and now there was little else to do but wait for traffic. Eliza immediately sat upon a skid of wood and began knitting while Louisa seemed content to stand back, arms folded and tight lipped, sternly watching the vendors prepare to the upcoming day.

"Did you bring something to read, Jacob?" Eliza asked brightly, smiling at him. Jacob nodded quickly and lowered his blue eyes, blushing. Her smile widened but she did not tease him. Jonah, however, seized the opportunity.

"We are ever so grateful that you did, Jacob! Otherwise you might never stop talking!" Jacob reached into his burlap sack to remove a book he had recently borrowed from the library in Lancaster, ignoring his brother.

"Leave him alone," Gabriel growled at Jonah. "At least he knows when to stay quiet."

"Oh, quiet yourself, Gabriel. If I can't tease Jacob, who can?"

"No one needs to bother Jacob," Eliza piped in pleasantly. "I think it's wonderful that he has such a disposition. It will take him far in life."

Jacob almost hugged his new sister. Instead he offered her a timid smile before looking back down at the pages before him.

"No one needs to be silent all the time," Louisa retorted. "Really, Jacob, how are you going to court anyone without learning how to speak?"

"That's enough!" Gabriel snapped. Everyone looked at him in surprise, including Jacob. "Jacob will marry when the time is right and he will speak to someone when he finds someone worthy of hearing his voice. Now leave him be!" Inexplicably, tears sprung into Jacob's eyes. Jonah looked abashed while Louisa looked contrite.

"Of course," Louisa mumbled, retreating to her spot against a post. Gabriel drew close to his younger brother.

"There is nothing wrong with you. You are patient, kind and you will make a just minister to our district one day. Don't let anyone tell you otherwise."

"Thank you, brother," Jacob murmured. Gabriel patted him reassuringly on the shoulder and went to join his wife. Jacob watched him walk away and wondered if that speech of confidence was actually for him or if Gabriel was just thinking to himself aloud.

The day got colder even as the sun fought to break through the ominous clouds. A storm was brewing and the market was suffering as a result. Only a few people had dared venture out as the temperatures dropped to a desolate, inconsolable place. It was the kind of day where even the marrow of the bones was chilled and could not be warmed under any circumstance. Most of the patrons were tourists passing through Amish country but a few neighboring communities stopped by to provide their support. Jacob was happy he had thought to bring along another book as he had barely had occasion to raise his eyes from the first one he had packed. Then fate mysteriously intervened.

It started as a shriek. Startled, Jacob looked up and blinked as an object came hurling at his head. Out of nowhere, a body slammed into his and he was belly down under the neighboring booth, Gabriel on top of him. A peal of child's laughter rang out, followed by a group chuckle and it was clear that whatever had occurred had merely been the act of a clumsy or mischievous child. But as Jacob rose put his hands down to raise his body up, his eyes locked upon a pair of light brown irises, crouched down like a preying tiger directly at his level. There was a face inches from his underneath the table, their lips almost touching one another. And suddenly Jacob was not in the din of the market any longer.

They skipped in a circle, the long grasses tickling their knees as the group picked up speed. The scent of wildflowers and herbs filled the air. Jacob's head was feeling light and he wasn't sure if it were as a result of the dizzying game or the beautiful eyes of his classmate, Grace which seemed to be fixated on his own. Even at the tender age of eight, Jacob recognized the impossible beauty of those orbs, a luminous, liquid brown, so light they seemed gold in the springtime sunlight. The round dance continued a few more laps until Grace herself "tripped" and landed the group into an unceremonious pile of young, panting bodies onto the lea. Yet through the reeds, Grace still stared at him and he at her. And not once did he feel the urge to look away in shyness.

"Jacob!" the eyes spoke. Quickly, Jacob lifted his head to stand and hit his skull against the booth, creating a sickening crack at the impact. His hand raised instinctively to his head.

"Oh! Are you all right?" She was at his side, grabbing his arm in aide. Jacob was immediately torn. He knew that he was not supposed to have this kind of contact with an outsider but this outsider was different…she was Grace.

"Uh…yes, thank you. Hello Grace," he mumbled, staring up at her. "How are you?"

Grace smiled that off-centered, charming grin which could disarm the angriest of bees.

"I'm well, Jacob. I'm so happy to see you here! I have been here a few times in the last months but you are never here when I come. I have been yearning for your goat cheese for years now and I finally had the courage to come around. Have you any for sale? Truly you can't find anything like your family's cheeses in the city."

Jacob nodded and before he could lead her around to the booth, he was looking up directly into Louisa's scowling face.

"Come along, Jacob," Louisa intervened, pulling him from Grace. "You're needed."

"But she wants – "Jacob protested.

"Eliza can help her," Louisa snapped. "Eliza! Help this woman!"

Louisa almost spat the word "woman" as she scathingly glared at Grace. Grace looked forlorn as she watched his sister-in-law shuffle him away. She slowly raised a gloved hand and smiled sadly as he looked back at her.

"Bye Jacob," she mouthed.

"You should know better, Jacob," Gabriel chided. They were back in their home, gathered by the warm hearth of the fire, counting their profits from the day. Jonah and Eliza looked up questioningly.

"Oh do tell! What could our patient Jacob possibly have done to earn trouble?" Eliza joked. "This I must hear!"

"Your brother-in-law was fraternizing with a fallen woman, a shunned member of this community," Louisa snapped. "Looking after her like some lost lamb. You should be ashamed of yourself, Jacob! You are just asking for trouble!"

"Who?" Eliza and Jonah chorused. "Which shunned woman?"

"That Beiler woman," Gabriel replied quietly. Eliza's eyes lit up.

"Lydia?" she squealed. "Oh how is she?"

Louisa's frown deepened into her characteristic scowl.

"No, the other one. Grace. Their poor, shamed parents. Can you imagine? Having two of your children living scandalously in the city? What are the odds of that occurring? It's no surprise they're in such poor health."

"Jacob, you saw Grace today?" Naomi, Jonah's twin looked up from kneading bread to address her younger brother. "How did she look? Is she well?"

Jacob nodded. Naomi and Grace had been very close before Grace had left the church. Naomi had been devastated when Grace had been exiled and she had never completely recovered. Probably no more than Jacob had.

"She said she was well," Jacob replied.

"You spoke to her?" their father was incensed from his rocking chair at the hearth. "Jacob, I expect better from you!"

"She was there to buy cheese!" Gabriel jumped in. "You cannot make a sale if you do not speak with the customers, papa."

Jacob looked gratefully at his brother.

"In the future, you let the women handle the women," their father muttered. All the siblings exchanged a secret smile, except, of course, Louisa.

"Jacob, what a pleasant surprise. How are you?" The bishop looked up from a pile of papers and smiled at the man in his doorway. "Please come in."

"Hello, Bishop. Is this an opportune time?"

"Of course! I don't get to see enough of you. Oh! Wait! I know what this is about! You're here to announce a betrothal!" The heavy set man clapped his hands together, his eyes lighting up with happiness. "Who is the lucky woman?"

Jacob shook his head quickly and averted his expressive blue eyes.

"No, Bishop. It's not a marriage announcement..." The bishop read Jacob's somber expression and his smile faded. He gestured at a simple chair across from his desk.

"Please sit down," he encouraged the younger man. Jacob obliged, still staring at the floor.

"Is something wrong, Jacob?"

"No...well..." Jacob paused, unsure of how to word what he wanted to say. He wished he had asked Gabriel for advice before doing something this inane. If his father found out...well it was too late now.

"Bishop, if someone were to be excommunicated, could they ever come back?" Sighing, Bishop Fisher sat back against the rigid chair and pushed his spectacles off the bridge of his nose, onto his receding hairline.

"Jacob, the idea behind rumspringa is for you to see what waits for you beyond the security of our community. That is why we look the other way when the young people go and experiment with different aspects of the world in which we don't engage before making the very important choice of being baptized. Once you are baptized, we expect that you have 'sowed your wild oats' so to speak. So Jacob, if you are having a crisis of faith, we can help you through community and prayer but if you choose to leave the Amish community now, it will be very difficult for you to return. Realistically, I would say nearly impossible. "

Jacob laughed, startling the man.

"I'm sorry, Bishop. I didn't mean to laugh. You needn't worry about me. I have no desire to go anywhere away from my family and land. I was asking about someone else." The bishop looked slightly more relaxed but curiosity gleamed in his eye.

"Could you give me the circumstances?" he asked. Jacob suddenly realized his mistake. The community was too close. There was no possible way that this meeting would not reach the ears of his family. He was acting like a foolish child, making this trip and asking ridiculous questions. Why would he assume that Grace would ever want to come back? She most likely loved her life in the city. She and may even be married already! Shame stained his cheeks crimson and Jacob stood suddenly.

"I'm sorry, Bishop. This was a silly thing for me to do. I made a mistake." Without waiting for an answer, Jacob hurried out of the small house and down the road toward his farm.

Jacob was about to vomit. He could feel the bile raising to his mouth, creating a pool of saliva under his tongue. *Don't get ill! You foolish, foolish man! What are you doing here?*

An elderly woman smiled kindly at him and handed him a paper bag from beside her seat.

"Motion sickness, honey?" she asked. Tentatively, Jacob accepted the bag. Then, to his horror, he retched into it. Surprisingly, after he was finished, he felt much better. The aging woman nodded knowingly.

"There you go. My grandson gets carsick too. He's only ten but I carry bags just in case. I didn't think people got carsick at your age," she told him.

"I've never been on a bus before," Jacob admitted. Her grinned widened and she nodded understandingly, taking in his simple, homespun clothing.

"Well that would explain it then. Just take deep breaths and try to relax. We'll be in Philadelphia in less than an hour." Jacob nodded and tried to heed her advice but his stomach would not settle. He imagined that had more to do with what he was doing than the actual bus ride itself. This was completely out of character for him. In fact, he could hardly believe what he was doing. He didn't know what he was hoping to accomplish but he also knew that since the day he had seen Grace in the market, he had been unable to think of anything but her. Her heart-warming smile was in the fireplace, her dark honey eyes were in the rays of sunlight streaking through the pines. He heard her voice in the chirping birds and once he thought he even saw her standing behind their barn but of course it had only been his mind playing tricks. He could not get her out of his head. He had to know if she was happy, if she thought of him or at least if she missed her life and her family in the district. Of course what he was doing was forbidden and if he were caught, he would be punished. But that would be the least of his problems. He would never hear the end of it from Louisa. Yet none of that seemed to matter. He would not rest until he knew that Grace was happy in her life. Even if that meant she was content without him.

As the older woman had predicted, less than an hour later, the bus was pulling into the hectic station in Philadelphia. Jacob had never seen such chaos. During rumspringa, he and Jonah had gone into town twice. Jonah had put on outsider clothing, smoked a cigarette and drank beer. Jacob had almost been sick from all of the foreign smells and the bustle. While he had accompanied his brother, he never felt the need to experiment with anything he did not know. There had never been any doubt that Jacob would be baptized. Unlike his peers, he had never felt the need go outside of is upbringing to see how good was their life. He recognized the purity in their way, the unity they had with nature and with each other. He couldn't imagine a life without the structural peace in which he had been reared. Jacob had always felt blessed by his birthright and respected the culture immensely. It was for all of these reasons that his underarms were soaked in perspiration at that moment, despite the crisp winter air. He nodded good-bye to his bus mate and slowly walked off the vehicle, his head swimming from all of the activity. *Stay focussed on your task, Jacob. You will be home before anyone realizes you are gone.* Once off the bus, he reached into the pocket of his plain brown pants and withdrew a scrap of paper. Then looking about, he spotted a taxi cab stop on the outskirts of the bustling station. Without hesitation, he made his way into a car and muttered the address written on the piece he was holding. The cabbie raised his eyebrow slightly at the sight of his passenger but made no comment at Jacob's outdated clothing.

"Is this your first time in Philly?" the man asked pleasantly, somehow feeling the need to put his obviously uncomfortable fare at ease. Jacob nodded quickly but stared out the window. His head was beginning to ache from all of the sights and sounds whizzing by the window.

"There's a lot of history here," the driver offered but when Jacob did not reply, he gave up and continued the relatively short trip to his destination. Jacob paid the charge and nodded before climbing onto the sidewalk. As the car drove away, he found himself looking back at the paper and then up at the apartment which he faced. He was in the right spot according to the phone book he had consulted at the Lancaster Library. This was Grace's home. For a moment, he considered aborting the mission all together and running back to the safety of Lancaster County. *But then you'll never know,* he told himself. And that was all the convincing he needed. He started up the steps and was inside the tiny entranceway, looking for her name on the intercom system. A teen boy walked out of the lobby and held the door open so Jacob slipped inside, rather than searching for the code. The phone book had declared Grace's apartment to be 401. Jacob opted for the stairs rather than the elevator. He reached the fourth floor and knocked on the door boasting 401 in scarred gold numbers. After a moment, he heard footsteps and a woman sing out.

"Coming!" Jacob swallowed and tried to prepare himself for coming face to face with the only woman who he had been able to speak with his entire life. But when the door flew open, it was not Grace. In Jacob's intense disappointment, he almost walked away, not realizing that he was looking at Lydia, Grace's younger sister.

"Jacob Miller! I don't believe my eyes!" she hollered. "Grace! You won't believe who is at our door!"

Jacob turned back to the doorway he was already departing, his eyes filled with hope at the sound of Grace's name.

"Is Grace here?" he asked, his voice no higher than a whisper. Lydia nodded eagerly and ushered him into the tiny apartment. Seconds later, Grace appeared in the hallway, her lava-like eyes wide with surprise.

"It really is you, Jacob! What – how...oh don't tell me you've been excommunicated!" Grace cried, rushing forward to embrace him in a hug. Not wanting to move but willing himself to do so, he stepped out of her friendly gesture and shook his head, color blushing his face with embarrassment.

"No...I...I came to see you, Grace," he said. "Is there any way we can speak? Just for a few moments?"

Lydia looked shocked but quickly nodded and said she was on her way out. She picked up a set of keys from the kitchen table and smiled briefly before flying out the door. Before she closed the door, she turned to Jacob, her eyes shiny.

"I understand that your brother wed Eliza Lapp. Please, if you find it in your heart, can you tell Eliza I think of her often?" Lydia did not wait for an answer and Jacob realized it was because she was about to cry. The door to the apartment closed and Grace smiled welcomingly at Jacob.

"Please, come and sit down. Can I offer you anything? A tea?" Jacob shook his head and sat down on the edge of an old velvet sofa.

"I can't tell you how wonderful it is to see you! I haven't been able to stop thinking about you since I saw you last week. I have been trying to find covert ways to see you and Naomi since I left. This has been my only fruitful attempt thus far. How is your sister?

Jacob nodded.

"She is well. She heard that I had seen you and asked the same. I believe she misses you very much, Grace." She smiled sadly.

"I miss her also. And I miss you, Jacob. You were my very first love." Jacob was stunned to hear the words. He had hoped, maybe even suspected that Grace had thought of him lovingly but he had always been far too bashful to find out if she held the same types of feelings for him. He felt like a weight had been lifted off his chest, a barbell which had resided upon him since the horrible day that Grace had left his life.

"Why don't you come back?" he asked her seriously. "Do you want to come back?"

Grace sat heavily back against the rocking chair in which she sat.

"Very much, Jacob but it is not that simple. If Lydia wanted to return, she would have a much easier time of it. She was never baptized so in theory, she never really left the church. She's basically on an extended rumspringa. I, on the other hand, have been baptized and I turned my back on my vows to our community."

"Why did you leave?" Jacob pressed before he could stop himself. He wasn't sure he wanted to hear the answer. He had always feared that she had fallen in love with an outsider. Grace's face fell.

"When Lydia began her rumspringa, it was just about a year after you and I had been baptized. Justine and Joseph had just gotten married and it was only Lydia and I left in the house with our parents. The workload doubled and I was fine with that but Lydia had always been willful. She began to act out and refuse to do the work. My parents' health had begun to fail at that point.

Suddenly, Lydia was not coming home at night and I would go looking for her and find her in cars with boys, high off marijuana, wearing skimpy clothing. I was only grateful my mother never had to witness anything of the sort or she would surely be dead by now of a heart attack. Night after night, I would drag Lydia home, pour cold water on her head and sober her up but this wasn't just a phase. I knew she was going to leave." Grace paused and looked up at Jacob.

"She is my little sister, Jacob. She is lost and naïve and doesn't know the ways of the world. She needed someone to protect her. She had no one..."

Jacob felt a lump grow in his throat. Grace was such an incredible sister. Would he do the same thing for Jonah or Naomi? He was ashamed but he knew that he would not. It took courage to do what she did for Lydia.

"How is Lydia doing now?" Jacob asked. He feared the answer.

"She is wonderful! She went to college and got a degree as a paralegal. She met a very nice man, a lawyer and I do believe he is going to propose any day now." Grace smiled but Jacob read the pain in her eyes.

"Do you want to come home?" Jacob asked again. Grace nodded slightly but changed her affirmative into a shrug.

"That's really not relevant, Jacob. I won't be welcomed back. I have learned to accept that fact. I knew what I was doing and this is my penance for making such a choice."

"You must speak to Bishop Fisher, Grace!" Jacob told her. She shook her head.

"You must go back home, Jacob and forget about me. If anyone finds out you were here..." She rose and went to guide him to the door.

"I can't tell you how wonderful it is to see you, Jacob. If you somehow find a way, tell your sister I miss her dearly. But don't put yourself into any trouble doing so." Instinctively, she reached out and embraced Jacob. Before he could stop himself, he had wrapped his own arms around her and relished the feeling of her closeness for one blissful moment. It might be the last time he ever had the opportunity.

"Good-bye, Jacob," she whispered in his ear and slowly closed the door, leaving him staring at it, troubled and confused.

"Bishop, is this an inopportune time?"

"Jacob! You left so quickly the other day, I thought it was something I had said!" the jovial man rose quickly from behind the scarred desk and hurried to greet Jacob at the door. "Please come in!"

Jacob moved further into the small office and sat before the elder, choosing his words carefully.

"Have you come to further discuss what we started the other day?" Jacob nodded.

"Sir, do you recall the Beiler sisters? Grace and Lydia?" The man frowned deeply, apparently troubled by the mention of their names.

"Yes," he replied slowly. "Why do you ask?"

"Grace would like to come home," Jacob answered simply. The Bishop began to shake his head at once but for the first time in his life, Jacob felt a rod of steel fuse into his spine and he sat up straight in his chair. He would not take no for an answer. Not this time.

"I do not think that is in the realm of possibility, son," the kindly man said. "Now if Lydia wanted to rejoin us, that might be possible since she has yet to be baptized however, it would be a process – "

"Lydia is very happy living in the outside world. Grace knows her place is here with us." The bishop continued to shake his head and Jacob felt his jaw clench, a motion that was foreign and unsettling to both men. Bishop Fisher seemed to recognize his anger at once and tried to diffuse the situation with logic.

"Jacob, what you are asking is out of the question. Grace Beiler chose to leave after she already committed herself to us. She not only abandoned our community, she left her own family to contend with an awful burden from both a labor and personal standpoint. Surely you cannot ignore those facts!" Jacob stared defiantly at Bishop Fisher.

"You don't know all of the facts, Bishop or you would change your mind," Jacob almost spat between clenched teeth. "Grace Beiler is an honorable woman and she belongs here with her people. She is willing to repent and undergo whatever punishment you deem fit to allow her back but please, Bishop, you must consider this!" Again, the Bishop shook his head, his eyes misty with sadness.

"This is not my decision to make, Jacob. Grace already made the decision for herself. There is nothing I can do. You must forget about Grace Beiler. There are many eligible women who would be very fortunate to be wed to you, Jacob. Please try to focus on what is feasible.

Grace Beiler is a dream." The Bishop stood up, indicating the conversation was done. Jacob felt familiar the lead weight of loneliness overwhelm his chest. He had known that this was apt to be the end result but he would have never forgiven himself if he had not given it a sincere chance. But he had failed. And Grace would never be there to untie his tongue as she had in childhood. As he slowly let himself outside into the cold winter afternoon, he somehow didn't see Grace's eyes in the sunlight for the first time since their encounter at the market.

Spring

The first day of warmth was a time for celebration among the Miller family. Although the temperatures had just barely climbed above freezing, it was enough to have melted the snow and cause a slushy mess for children to stomp around while the men bravely retired their heavy wool coats and the women dared leave the wash on the line all day without fear of freezing the handmade fabrics. Even Louisa seemed to be in a good mood as the brand new baby buds dripped snowflakes into puddles of water and caught the golden sunrays in their reflections. Louisa had just discovered she was with child and for the first time that anyone could remember, she was actually smiling. It was a lovely smile, in fact and quite infectious. In fact, she often had kind words to say. The only one unaffected by the magic the season change appeared to bring about was Jacob. Not even Jonah and Eliza had been able to lift him out of the depth of his despair since his meeting with the Bishop. Of course Jacob had not disclosed the reason for his mood but instead thrown himself into work. When he was forced to be in the presence of others, he ensured he had a plethora of reading material at his side as to avoid any potential conversation. The day that the warmth finally remembered their district, Jacob had been up well before dawn, milking the cows as he always did. He wanted to be done the majority of his chores before retreating to the barn and hiding in the loft. He had actually acquired an interesting mystery from the library and he was eager to read the ending. As the morning hour turned close to noon, Jacob hurried out of the chicken coop with a basket full of eggs and almost slipped in the mud near the pig pen. Steadying himself before he lost the day's yolks, he grabbed onto the fence with his free hand and looked up. Directly on the other side of the gate was the most beautiful woman he had ever seen. Her long blonde hair was loose and hanging about her gray, ankle-length dress, under a matching gray bonnet, slightly blowing in the gentle breeze. Her mouth was turned up into a crooked smile, off centered but intensely charming and as it always did, sunlight caught the molten brown of her eyes, melting the sadness out of Jacob from the moment his forlorn irises met them.

"Grace!" he whispered, hushed and looked around figuratively. "What are you doing here?"

Her beam widened.

"This is my home, Jacob, and I've come to thank you for helping me find my way back. And also I would like to inform you that my parents have painted their gate blue."

Late Winter

No one could have prepared her for the man standing on the other side of the door but it truly was Bishop Fisher and he was there to speak to her. Lydia had conveniently disappeared, extremely uncomfortable by the reminder of the past she had left behind but Grace had welcomed the Bishop into the cozy apartment, offering him a hot tea and they had talked for hours, about Lydia, about her parents, about why she had left and of course, about Jacob. After their discussion, the Bishop told her that he wanted to have her return but he needed to discuss it with the ministers first. Of course, the process would be long and require intense atonement for what she had done. There was one more subtlety; that she would sincerely consider Jacob as a husband. Grace had smiled and nodded. After he left, she had shaken her head and laughed. How could the Bishop know that the main reason she had wanted to return for so many years was to be with Jacob?

REBECCA'S RUMSPRINGA

ALANA MILLER

Rebecca stared out of the window of her bedroom, the one she shared with her younger brothers and sisters. The fields rolled before her, barren now that the harvest was over. She had begged her parents to delay the Rumspringa, until after the harvest at least, even though her birthday had just passed this summer. She had tried to convince them to let her stay, but they insisted she go.

"Rebecca, would you come here please?" her mother called from the kitchen.

"Yes, Momma." She called back and deposited her knitting into the basket at the corner of her room. Rebecca fixed her skirts, brushing off yarn hairs that were attracted to the plain navy color. She walked down the hall and into the kitchen. Her mother pulled a fresh pie out of the oven and set it on a potholder on the table.

"Rebecca, can you go down into the cellar and fetch me another can of apples? Then go and fetch your siblings from the barn for supper."

"Yes, Momma." Rebecca said, and pulled on her boots. She stalked across the ground to the barn as the sun began to dip behind the hills and trees. She could hear her younger siblings screeching and laughing in the hayloft. She pulled open the door and smelled the sweet hay and manure.

"Come on, kids. Momma says its supper time." She called to the hayloft. She heard their muffled giggles and the boards sigh as they shifted their weight behind the hay bales.

"Alright, I guess I'll just have to eat all the potatoes and carrots from the roast Momma made. I know how much Anna and Naomi and Fannie love those little sweet carrots. Too bad they're not out here." Rebecca called and turn to leave. She heard her young siblings scramble down the ladder.

They raced past her into the house. She walked behind and lingered for a few more seconds, hoping to catch a glimpse of the neighbor boy, Joshua Hostetler. He was a cute boy, nearing manhood, and possibly looking a wife soon. She would catch him glancing at her when they were both working their respective fields with their families, or when they passed each other after services. Of course, she would glance back, but sparingly.

They sat around the dinner table, her father said the blessing, they ate. Rebecca's mind wandered as she picked absentmindedly at her plate. She wondered what she would see, who she would meet. She had heard about the outside world, how crass and improper it could be. She felt her stomach drop and twist with nerves.

Rebecca changed into her nightgown and sighed. She would miss her bed, the secret cat only the kids knew about who lived in the attic, the smell of hay.

"So, Rebecca, thought about anyone dreamy lately?" Anna laid sprawled across Rebecca's bed and flipped through the pages of her diary.

"Anna, you little snot!" Rebecca lunged and snatched the diary out of danger.

"What? It's fun to read." Anna slid into her own bed.

"That's rude, Anna! You're supposed to respect others and their feelings," Rebecca said, throwing her pillow at Anna.

"Well, if you marry Joshua Hostetler, then I can't marry his younger brother. When I come of age, of course," Anna said, brushing her hair back.

"You are too young to think about such things now. As the youngest, you'll have the worst choice anyways," Rebecca teased and brushed Anna's hair. Naomi, Fannie, and Maggie sit on the bed.

"Tells us about what you and Joshua," Naomi said. Rebecca smiled softly and started to braid Anna's hair.

"Me and Joshua will live in the old King house, that beautiful one with the large attic room and the big kitchen. We'll have so many children, eight or nine. I'll make quilts for all of them and have lots of grandchildren and be the best mother and wife and grandmother. I can't imagine anything better than just being happy and in good health with a good husband." Rebecca said. Her mind wandered to her marriage day.

She said good night to her siblings and tucked them all into bed. She crept downstairs and watched her parents sleeping for just a moment. She crept back upstairs and knelt by her bed and said her prayers.

Dear God, please watch over my family. Thank you for giving me this day and thank you for giving me tomorrow. Please let my siblings grow up strong and let my parents grow old. Please let me bless my family with lots of children and grandchildren. Please bless all my sisters with good husbands and my brothers with good wives. Thank you for this good harvest and please let next year be just as good. In your name I pray, Amen.

She got into bed and began to write in her diary. The candle light fluttered and flickered as she wrote. She wrote about her day, about tending her mother's herb garden, about the socks she was darning. She wrote about Joshua, as well, just a little bit. Then she blew out the candle and snuggled under the thick handmade quilt.

Rebecca rose before the sun, just like every other day. She dressed quickly, pulling on warm thick socks against the cool fall. She crept down the stairs slowly. Her mother sat in the rocking chair by the front door. She grabbed her mother's shoulder.

"Are you ready to go?" They both looked out the window as the sun began to color the sky.

"Yes, Momma. I'm not sure if I really want to go," Rebecca said softly. Upstairs, she could hear tiny feet stirring as her brothers and sisters woke up.

"It'll be good for you. You need to see something other than the same old farm and same old people. You don't feel restless now, but you will if you don't take this opportunity. Go be young and free so you can come home and start a family and be a good wife," her mother said, squeezing Rebecca's hand.

"So you went on your own Rumspringa, then Momma?" Rebecca knelt by her mother's chair.

"Aye. It was actually a bit boring. I went up the road to the town and stayed with a very nice English family. It was summer, and I tended their children and their house while the parents were working. They were good Christian folks. It was refreshing to get out, and see how the world works outside. But I'm sure things have changed since then," her mother said, reminiscing.

"Do you want me to get you a gift while I'm out," Rebecca joked.

"Maybe just a new recipe or some new fabric for a quilt. I'm thinking something with purple or green in it."

"Alright, Momma. I'm going to go finish packing." She kissed her mother's hand and stood. Her siblings rushed down the stairs and into the kitchen. Rebecca walked back up the stairs and finished packing her knapsack; her diary, an extra dress, two extra pairs of socks, and an extra bootlace.

She said goodbye to family when the sun finally rose. She hugged her siblings tightly. Her father hugged her tighter and longer.

"I'll miss you, little flower" he muttered.

"I'll miss you, too, Poppa," she said back into his shoulder. She kissed her mother's cheek and hugged her tightly, too.

Then she set off. She hefted her knapsack onto her shoulder and set off down the old dirt road. As she passed the Hostetler farm, Joshua waved her down from his porch. He shouldered his own pack and jogged across the yard to the road.

"Hi, Rebecca. Mind if I walk with you?"

"Not at all. How are you, Joshua?" She shifted her bag.

"I'm doing well. Let me take that for you." He grabbed her knapsack and slung it over his other shoulder.

"Are you excited," she asked, putting her hands in her pockets.

"Yeah, a little. I want to go and see a movie and taste popcorn." Rebecca glanced at him, out of the corner of her eye. He was handsome, in his dark plain shirt. She didn't feel quite pretty enough standing next him in her plain black dress. She wanted him to notice her, but she didn't want to act like those English girls who wore too much rogue and too little clothing.

"That sounds fun," she remarked lightly. Her stomach fluttered with nervous butterflies.

"What do you plan on doing?" He looked straight at her now. *Straight and honest like a good Amish man,* she thought.

"I'm going to find some fabric for my mother, and maybe some toys for my siblings. My father didn't want anything, but I'm going to find him a new book."

"Rebecca, this is a chance at freedom, not a market trip," he laughed. She liked his laugh, deep and hearty.

"Aye, I know. But I don't really want to go on this trip to begin with, so I figured I would make it a practical trip," she sulked.

"You are a proper Amish woman, if there was ever one," he chuckled and adjusted their packs.

They met Sarah at the edge of the community. They stood for a moment under the gate. Rebecca rubbed her fingers together, trying to rub a little warmth back into them.

"Good morning, Sarah." Joshua said politely.

"Good morning, Joshua. Are we ready to go," she replied. She hefted her pack high onto her shoulder and set off down the road towards town.

"I guess we're going," Rebecca muttered. She and Sarah had been friends long ago, but when Sarah made her intention clear of leaving the community, their friendship faltered. Sarah had been shunned and Rebecca had not been allowed to even talk to her friend. Rebecca had wanted to be there, to help her friend through what must've been a hard time to come to the decision to leave the only community she knew.

They tromped down the road side by side. Cars zoomed by, some honked, some had teens leaning out windows and yelling at them. Someone even threw trash at them. Rebecca took Sarah's hand. She didn't take Joshua's. When they made it into town, the sun was high overhead. Between them, they had a little over $70.

"Do you know where we should go? Or what we're supposed to do?" Rebecca looked between Sarah and Joshua.

"We find a place called a hotel. We get a room for the night. Then tomorrow I'm going to the city. You two can do whatever," Sarah said disdainfully.

"What's in the city?" Joshua fixed a stern look at Sarah.

"A publishing house. I'm going to be a writer, a famous writer. I'll cut my hair short and wear pants." Sarah remarked. She shifted her bag and stalked off down the street. She glanced over her shoulder at Rebecca and Joshua, then ducked into a restaurant. Joshua looked at Rebecca and shrugged. They followed her down the sidewalk and into the restaurant. As they sat down at a table, Rebecca noticed the strange looks they garnered. The young waitress who took their orders gave them curious glances from across the restaurant. Her name tag said Helen. She was short and petite, with long blond wavy hair pulled back into a high ponytail.

"I'm sorry to stare, but you're Amish, right?" The waitress looked at them, with the same curiosity of a child seeing a lion at the zoo for the first time. She had a strange accent, drawing out some of the vowels.

"Yes, we're out on Rumspringa, which is like a journey Amish youth take before becoming full-fledged members of the community." Rebecca smiled sweetly at the girl.

"That's pretty cool. A lot of local kids just go to the big city for a couple months before coming back here. Some of them go to college and meet people, then come back and settle down. "

"What do they do in the big city?" Sarah said, her eyes shining brightly.

"Party usually. They just do stupid stuff and pretend that they're adults. It's boring, really." Helen shrugged.

"So, what do you local kids do?" Joshua said, giving the waitress a strange half-smile. Rebecca felt a strange thread of jealousy. *He's never given me a smile like that,* she thought. She considered pouting, but she was an adult now, she didn't need to pout.

"We go to the library and the movies and the mall in the next town over. Sometimes I hit up a barn party on the other side town. Just every now and then. It's kind of fun." Helen shrugged again.

After they ate, Sarah dragged Rebecca towards the back of the restaurant, towards Helen.

"Helen, right? I'm Sarah and this Rebecca. I was wondering, I don't want to impose, but do you know where there's a store nearby? I don't think we brought enough clothes and we just need to pick up something to blend in a little better."

"Oh, yeah. There's a place just a few doors down. If you want to wait just a little longer, I'll be off work and I can get my friends Alex and Tiffany to help us out. Alex loves shopping," She said, trailing off a little at the end.

"Oh, thank you, but on second thought, I think we can manage on our own," Rebecca stuttered nervously.

"Are you sure? I seriously don't mind," Helen said.

"Yes, we'll be fine. We don't need to impose on your charity," Rebecca said, more forceful now.

"Alright. I'm not very familiar with how things work out in the boonies up here, but I'm from the South. Besides racism and comfort food, we have hospitality. That means we take care of our guests." She took her apron and flung it on the counter.

"Delilah, I'm taking my lunch now!" Helen grabbed Sarah and Rebecca's wrists and dragged them out of the restaurant. Joshua scrambled after them. Helen pulled out, what Rebecca assumed was her phone, and tapped on the rectangular glass repeatedly.

"Alex, I need you to drop everything and meet us downtown now." She paused. "No, fashion emergency. And get Tiffany down here too." She paused again. "Yes, yes. I'll see you in a moment." She pushed the rectangle back into her pants pocket.

She pulled the two girls after her, down the smooth sidewalk. Joshua jogged to keep up with them. Helen pushed the two girls into a small corner shop that was mostly windows. The shop was packed with clothing racks that erupted fabric of all shapes, sizes, and colors. Even from all the stories and scant images, Rebecca could still barely believe all the colors and fabrics stretching before her.

Helen set about pulling article after article from the racks. A bored looking youth manned the counter. Rebecca couldn't tell much about the youth; they had short chopped up colored hair, and scary spikes through their eyebrows and ears. Rebecca was intimidated by them. But they made her feel overexposed; that typical English teen made her feel so out place. Joshua watched as Helen piled clothes on both of the girls. She then pushed them into tiny cubicles and closed the doors.

"Start trying those things on. I had to guess at a lot of your sizes, since those dresses don't do you girls any justice," Helen yelled and threw the piles over the top of the door.

Rebecca looked through everything. *How does anybody get anything done when they have to spend so much time picking out clothes and then putting them on,* she thought to herself as she stripped out of her dress. She picked up the first thing that caught her eye and glared at it. It was purple and strangely strappy. She couldn't decide if it was a sweater or a scarf.

"Helen? I think I need some help," Sarah called from her closet. Rebecca heard the chuckle from Helen.

"Luckily the cavalry has arrived, ladies," Helen chuckled and opened the door a crack.

"Rebecca, honey, this is Alex. She's going to help you get into those things. I didn't even think about the whole culture shock thing." Helen shoved a tall, slim girl into the changing room. The girl was dark skinned and had curly hair. Rebecca wanted to know how she got her hair to curl like that. Alex had a small gold stud piercing in the side of her nose.

"Hi, I'm Alex." She held out her hand to Rebecca. Rebecca took it and shook her hand like she had seen men do.

"Here, let me help you into that. Aren't you going to take that off?" Alex eyed the slip Rebecca wore.

"No? This is like our, uh, underwear." Rebecca blushed fiercely.

"Oh, okay. Then try this on instead." Alex handed her a bright blue sweater that Rebecca did like over the purple one. They spent hours cramming themselves into strange clothes. Rebecca felt like the English girls spoke a whole different language as they passed clothes back and forth to Sarah and Rebecca.

Size 4 instead of 6...
Grunge, not punk...
No, darker...
No, lighter...
Pastels...
More sparkles, Less sparkles...

At the end of the ordeal, Rebecca and Sarah muttered to each other and counted their money. The number crept higher and higher. Rebecca felt like her heart was going to explode and her stomach twisted in knots. They stepped up to the counter, ready to face the music. Helen pushed her way between them.

"Girls, put your damn money away right now." She slapped a plastic card on the counter top and glared over her shoulder at the two girls who clutched their money nervously.

"But, Helen –," Rebecca started.

"No. Away with it." The rectangle was swiped in the machine and the cashier bagged their clothes up. Joshua was leaning wearily against the wall. Rebecca picked up her bag of clothes. The plastic felt greasy and slick on her palm. Shame crept up her neck. As they exited the store, Rebecca wanted to turn and run.

"Thank you, Helen, for your generosity. We'll be on our way now." Rebecca looked down to avoid eye contact with Helen. Helen grabbed her shoulder.

"Let's go. My place is just a couple blocks away."

"Helen, we can't impose on you anymore," Joshua laid his hand over Helen's.

"It's not imposing. When you make new friends, you're supposed to take care of them. Tonight that means going to my house, sleeping in my beds, and eating my food." She winked at Joshua and squeezed Rebecca's arm gently. Alex pulled up to the curb in her car, a silver 4 door car.

They piled in; Helen sat in the front passenger seat and the other 4 into the back. Tiffany and Sarah sat squished against one door. Rebecca sat between the other door and Joshua. Joshua's leg pressed against hers snuggly. When they took corners too sharply, because Alex was not a very good driver, he would press harder against her. Rebecca could feel the heat in her face. She kept her eyes carefully fixed on studying the pattern of the back of the seat. Then he leaned over, on purpose.

"How do you feel about your first car ride," he whispered.

"It's a little hot and cramped. Do you think all car rides are this way?" He chuckled lowly in her ear. She could feel his breath on her neck. Her faced flared brilliant red as her thoughts began to race. *I wonder what it would feel like to kiss him at this moment...* She mentally chastised herself and sent a prayer to God, asking for forgiveness of her lust.

They stopped outside a two-story house. It was pastel yellow. There were large windows all across the front. Alex pulled into the driveway and parked. Rebecca fumbled with the door latch before finally squeezing it enough to open the door. She slid out of the car and onto the front lawn gracelessly. She straightened her skirts and brushed some wrinkles out. Her hands felt clammy and shook a little. She grabbed her old knapsack and her new plastic bag filled with new clothes.

"Your house is very large," Joshua observed. His eyes darted all around the house.

"Really? This is like a smaller house on this block. It's got like 3 bedrooms and only 1 bathroom. The back yard is a nice size though, good for a small or medium dog," Tiffany shrugged and walked up the stairs of the front porch.

"You lock the doors around here?" Rebecca stared at the chain of keys Tiffany picked through.

"Yeah? You don't?" Tiffany looked at Rebecca like she had just sprouted feathers. Rebecca had never needed to lock doors at home; they were a community and no one needed to steal anything.

They all pushed through the door. Sarah, Joshua, and Rebecca stood in the doorway, watching the three young women. Tiffany turned lights on all over the place. Rebecca played with one of the switches and watched the light flick on and off above her. Alex and Helen stand in the kitchen, tapping away on their phones.

"Okay, I'll get the girls set up in the spare bed. But where will we put sweet little Joshy?" Alex said and winked at Joshua. His face turned scarlet. Rebecca couldn't help but glare at her. Tiffany bumped her arm.

"Don't worry, she's teasing. She's very involved with her long-time boyfriend Thomas. They'll probably get married someday, but she's having too much fun being young," Tiffany whispered. She offered Rebecca a sweet smile. Rebecca and Sarah trudged up the stairs after Alex. She opened a door at the end of the hall, second door on the left, Rebecca noted.

"Sorry, there's only one bed. I hope that's not an issue." Alex glanced between the two girls.

"No, sisters share bed until one of the gets married." Sarah said and slid past Alex. Alex grabbed Rebecca's arm though.

"I saw your face downstairs. If I was out of line, I'm sorry. But if you would like, I can show you a thing or two about wooing a prospective male." Alex smiled sweetly down at Rebecca. Rebecca offered her an awkward half-smile and edged into the bedroom. They spread their new cloths out on the bed.

"These cloths are so weird. They don't feel... right," Rebecca said and ran her fingers across the clothes. Sarah shrugged and stripped out of her dress. She pulled on her new clothes quickly. Sarah looked in the mirror above the dresser and pulled off her prayer cap.

"I like them." Sarah left the room. Rebecca gaped at her. Then she stripped off her own clothes and pulled on the black slacks and baby blue sweater. She looked in the mirror too. She saw a young girl staring back, one who was afraid of her future. The stark white prayer cap covered her brown hair. She also removed the cap and her hair fell into a long braid down her back.

Rebecca walked down the stairs slowly. Her gut knotted when she thought of what Joshua would think of her. Only married couples saw a woman's hair. She walked into the kitchen, in only her sock covered feet. Sarah and Tiffany sat at the table, talking about her hair. Helen opened a rectangular box and Rebecca felt her stomach grumble.

"Here, this is the most American food that has ever existed. Pizza!" She held a slice covered in pepperoni out to her. Rebecca took a bite out of the cheesy triangle. The hot cheese burned her tongue but tasted amazing. She smiled and nodded at Helen's expectant face. But pizza was forgotten in a snap; Joshua walked in a plain white t-shirt and dark blue jeans. Rebecca's face flared again and she looked down, away from him.

"Rebecca..." He didn't finish that thought. The unspoken intimacy between them, felt by only them, created tension that pervaded the room. Alex cleared her throat loudly.

"So, there's a party going on tonight, if you guys want to hit it up? We can finish some pizza and get out there," Helen said, leaning heavily on the table.

"Yeah, let's go!" Sarah lit up.

"Okay, that's settled. Let's go get ready, ladies. Joshua, you look great already." Alex winked at him again and herded the girls up the stairs. Joshua's eyes never left Rebecca.

Upstairs, in Alex's bedroom, Sarah and Rebecca were subject to poking and prodding, being stuffed into strange tight dresses. Rebecca pulled on the strange tights under her short dress. They made her miss her thick, comfy socks. The English girls smeared her face with make-up; reddened her lips and lined her eyes in thick black lines. They pulled her hair and curled it and brushed it. Rebecca couldn't recognize herself after they were done with her.

She walked down the stairs holding onto Helen's arm. Joshua looked up at her from the bottom of the stairs. He looked a little disappointed, but he didn't take his eyes off her. Rebecca felt a small sliver of pride knowing that Joshua only had eyes for her. They piled into Alex's car and drove off to the party. Rebecca felt a little more comfortable this time, sitting next to Joshua. *I'm almost in his lap, What am I supposed to do if something like that happens?*

They walked up to the barn. Joshua was still taller than her in her ridiculous shoes that squeezed her toes and made her ankles feel weak. *Or maybe Joshua is why my ankles feel weak,* she thought to herself with a secret smile. Loud music pounded and Rebecca could feel it in her heart, like a second heartbeat. Inside, there were barely any lights. Rebecca could see teens dancing with each other; it looked like animals mating. She wanted to turn and leave. Helen pushed a plastic cup into her hand and demanded she drink it.

The alcohol burned her throat. She gagged and coughed. Joshua was whisked away into the party by several guys that Alex and Helen knew. Rebecca leaned against a wall and watched teens kiss and grind and drink. *This isn't the place for me...* Someone grabbed her arm and startled her.

"It's just me," Joshua screamed over the music. Rebecca smiled at him. He took her hand and led her outside.

"Sorry, I just needed some air. Are you having fun?" He looked her up and down. He smelled of alcohol.

"No, but this will be a story to tell my kids and grandchildren," she chuckled.

"Let's take a walk." He took her hand again and led her down road. They walked for a few minutes. Then Joshua slipped his hand over her rear. She pushed him away forcefully.

"Joshua!" Rebecca stared at Joshua, her heart pounded against her ribs. Her stomach churned from the alcohol.

"I'm sorry. This is just a, a misunderstanding!" He glanced around. Panic was setting in and shone in his eyes.

"What do you mean, a misunderstanding? You've brought me out here in the middle of the night and for what? To catch our death of cold? And you gave me that nasty poison, for what? To drag me down into the filth and sin with Sarah? And then you try to start something that I gave no intention of wanting!" Rebecca felt the panic rise in her throat.

"I'm sorry, Rebecca. I didn't mean to. It was a stupid dare from those English boys I was hanging out with. I just wanted a chance to be alone with you." Joshua looked down. Even in the dark, Rebecca saw the blush creep across his face.

"Why? If you had wanted to talk to me, you could've said so!" Rebecca yelled, exasperated.

"I just didn't know how to talk to you. And those English boys were trying to convince me to 'make my move' on you." Joshua shoved his hands in his pockets.

"Oh Joshua," Rebecca sighed. The cold was starting to chill her.

Rebecca held the coat tightly against her body. She felt so small at that moment. *God, please watch over me and Joshua for what we are about to do,* she prayed silently. She shivered slightly.

"Joshua, come on. Let's go. We can walk to town in just a few hours," Rebecca said, holding out her hand. Joshua took it, his large calloused hand enveloped her smaller one. Her heart pounded even harder now.

"You shouldn't be walking in those ridiculous shoes," he remarked. She was wearing ridiculous shoes. "But you do look nice tonight," he added. She blushed and looked away from him.

"Do you think we'll be okay, being out here on our own?" She left out the rest of her thought. *Do you think we'll okay without a chaperone?*

"I hope so, Rebecca. This has got to be the worst Rumspringa in the history of ever." Joshua squeezed her hand gently. She hoped her heart wouldn't jump out of her chest.

"The first Rumspringa was probably terrible," she said, with a chuckle," Because back then, the English lived just like us, so it was probably just boring to leave." She laughed.

"That is a very good point," he said back.

"Have you thought what you'll do when we get back?"

"Yeah. I'm going to apprentice under Miles Yoder and learn how to care for cattle and such. I think it would be easier to have livestock than to tend a field." She watched him out of the corner of her eye. She liked seeing his eyes sparkle and she could see the thoughts racing through his head. She had much of the same thoughts constantly racing through her head.

"Have you thought about who you would like to marry, someday," Rebecca said, trying to be casual, nonchalant.

"Yeah, just a passing thought or two. You?" He squeezed her hand again. She squeezed his back. Her feet started to hurt now and her fingers had started to burn from the cold.

"Yeah, every now and then." She said, looking at him. He stopped and looked at her. Their English clothes were dirty from tromping through the dark woods. She felt tired in ways she couldn't have imagined.

"Rebecca," he whispered. It wasn't a question or a statement. He said it like he just wanted to hear her name from his own two lips.

"Yes, Joshua?" She felt like there were swarms off bees in her belly, buzzing and fluttering.

"Who do you think about when you think about your future?" He stepped ever so slightly closer.

"You really want to know?" She smiled up at him. She loved his jaw, his grey-green eyes she could barely see in the dark, the way his hair curled and the shadow of facial hair that had begun to grow.

"Yes."

"Kiss me," she whispered. Her heart pounded so hard against her ribs. His hands crept under her coat, but stayed on her waist. He pulled her close. She slipped up onto tiptoes, trying to get closer faster. But her ridiculous shoes had other plans. She stumbled into him.

"Sorry, I don't know what I thinking." She giggled and rested her head on his shoulder.

"I do," he said. His rough fingers turned her chin up slightly. Her breath caught in her throat as he leaned forward ever so slightly. It felt like time stopped in that moment. Her heart beat once, twice and then his lips finally brushed against hers. It was so soft, so gentle, so short. *Again*, she thought.

"Again? You sure?" He joked.

"I didn't mean to say that out loud," she laughed and clutched his jacket," do you think we'll get in trouble? I don't think that was allowed."

"If nobody knows, then I think we'll be okay."

Joshua put his arms around her and hugged her tight. She hugged him back.

"When we get back, we'll have to do things proper. All the courtship traditions and such," Joshua said, "Do you think your father will allow me to marry you?"

"Probably. He thinks your father is a good man, and will give me over willingly. I do like how the English move through courtship. That Alex girl has been with her boyfriend for many years, but they didn't have to hide it or ask any permission of anyone. And they divorce all the time!" Rebecca shivered in her coat.

"I know! Imagine if any of the women did that at home! The shunning, the outrage," Joshua said dramatically.

"Imagine if we went through courtship like the English! Kissing on the first meeting, married by the third, having children by the time we were together three months, then splitting up by our first anniversary," Rebecca draped herself against Joshua. Her feet hurt in those shoes, but she knew if she took them off she would only be colder.

"We wouldn't split up. You're stuck with me now, Miss Fisher." Joshua stopped and looked at her again. "If you'll have me, that is." His eyes were full of hope.

"Are you asking me to marry you, Joshua Hostetler?" Rebecca was cold and hot all at once. Tonight had been such a strange night.

"Aye," he whispered. Her cold fingers grasped his.

"Then aye, I'll have you," She whispered back.

"Then let's get back to town and back home."

"First, another kiss?" she asked quietly.

"Of course, my dear," he replied softly. His lips brushed against hers so softly and gently. She didn't know if it had been the alcohol in her body or love, but she leaned further into it. The kiss edged from adorable and chaste to passionate and fiery. Rebecca understood why English girls kissed boys all the time; it felt hot and intense. She felt like time stopped around them. She no longer felt her cold fingers and cold toes. It was addictive to be so close to him, to be just the two of them in that moment. He pushed her away gently.

"I'm sorry. Forgive me, I acted improperly," She whispered. Shame flared across her face. She couldn't bring her eyes to meet his. He chuckled slightly.

"So did I. Let's get back to town, you're freezing." He kissed her forehead. He took her hand and led her back to town and to the warm beds waiting for them.

"Hey, Joshua, want to hear something really funny?" Rebecca pushed her face against his arm.

"Sure," he chuckled.

"I'm not wearing any underwear!" Rebecca giggled.

"Come on, you need to sober up." He wrapped an arm around her shoulder and they walked home.

The next day, they all stood outside the restaurant. Joshua held Rebecca's hand tightly. They had changed back into their Amish clothing, their normal clothing. Sarah looked so strange from when she had arrived just a few days earlier; she had shorn her long brown hair so short, into what Alex called a 'pixie' cut, and was wearing typical English clothing. Rebecca was sad to see her friend leave, but was happy she had found where she belonged. *Dear God, please watch Sarah as she walks a different path,* she prayed silently.

"Okay, you crazy kids. Be safe, don't fall off your horses and such. I'll be stopping by in the future to see your wedding, and oh- meeting your children!" Helen sobbed a little. Rebecca hugged her close.

"Aye, we'll be waiting for you. We'll send out invitations with all the dates and such. Amish have very intensive courtship traditions." Rebecca wiped a stray tear from her own face.

"I hope we're invited, too," Alex asked and hugged Rebecca tightly and then hugged Joshua tightly.

"Of course. Everyone will be invited. It'll be the biggest wedding, with Amish and English sitting down and celebrating our marriage," Joshua exclaimed and hugged Rebecca tightly. She couldn't help but giggle.

"Now get out of here! Go get to courting!" Helen sniffled and pushed them gently. They walked down the road, hand in hand. Their future was bright, and almost in their grasp. Just a few more steps down the road. Rebecca saw their lives playing out in front of them, the happiest in Joshua's face on their wedding day, the purity of the wedding night, the joy of their first year together and of their first child. On and on, their lives would be happy and peaceful. Rebecca was content to know that she was on her path and she had the man of her dreams next to her for every step of the journey.